"You Can't Make Me Marry You."

"Lilly, Lilly." Nick continued the gentle glide of his thumb across her throat. "I'd like to haul your pretty little butt down to the courthouse right now. You're having my baby. Letting you set the date is being a whole lot more generous than I'm feeling." Abruptly he stopped caressing her. "Want to push me?"

She didn't respond.

"So how about it? What kind of ceremony should we have? And when? The choice is yours."

Tears shimmered on the length of her eyelashes, but he didn't relent. His moral code didn't allow him to back down from what was important. And nothing ever had been more important than this. No child of his was going to grow up without a mother *and* a father. He took care of what was his. No matter the cost.

"Choice?" she echoed. "What kind of choice is that?"

"The only one you're going to get."

Dear Reader,

Merry Christmas from Silhouette Desire—where you're guaranteed powerful, passionate and provocative love stories that feature rugged heroes and spirited heroines who experience the full emotional intensity of falling in love!

The always-wonderful Cait London is back with this December's MAN OF THE MONTH, who happens to be one of THE BLAYLOCKS. In *Typical Male,* a modern warrior hero is attracted to the woman who wants to destroy him.

The thrilling Desire miniseries TEXAS CATTLEMAN'S CLUB concludes with *Lone Star Prince* by Cindy Gerard. Her Royal Princess Anna von Oberland finally reunites with the dashing attorney Gregory Hunt who fathered her child years ago.

Talented Ashley Summers returns to Desire with *That Loving Touch,* where a pregnant woman becomes snowbound with a sexy executive in his cabin. The ever-popular BACHELOR BATTALION gets into the holiday spirit with *Marine under the Mistletoe* by Maureen Child. *Star-Crossed Lovers* is a Romeo-and-Juliet-with-a-happy-ending story by Zena Valentine. And an honorable cowboy demands the woman pregnant with his child marry him in Christy Lockhart's *The Cowboy's Christmas Baby.*

Each and every month, Silhouette Desire offers you six exhilarating journeys into the seductive world of romance. So make a commitment to sensual love and treat yourself to all six for some great holiday reading this month!

Enjoy!

Joan Marlow Golan
Senior Editor, Silhouette Desire

Please address questions and book requests to:
Silhouette Reader Service
U.S.: 3010 Walden Ave., P.O. Box 1325, Buffalo, NY 14269
Canadian: P.O. Box 609, Fort Erie, Ont. L2A 5X3

The Cowboy's
Christmas Baby
CHRISTY LOCKHART

Silhouette

Desire

Published by Silhouette Books

America's Publisher of Contemporary Romance

SILHOUETTE BOOKS

ISBN 0-373-76260-7

THE COWBOY'S CHRISTMAS BABY

Copyright © 1999 by Christine Pacheco

Visit us at www.romance.net

Printed in U.S.A.

Books by Christy Lockhart

Silhouette Desire

Hart's Baby #1193
Let's Have a Baby! #1212
The Cowboy's Christmas Baby #1260

Previously published as Christine Pacheco

Silhouette Desire

The Rogue and the Rich Girl #960
Lovers Only #1054
A Husband in Her Stocking #1113

CHRISTY LOCKHART

married her real-life hero, Jared, who proved to her that dreams really do come true. They live in Colorado with their two children, Raymond and Whitney.

Christy remembers always wanting to be a writer. She even talked her elementary school librarian into "publishing" her books. She notes always preferring romances because they're about that special moment when dreams are possible and the future is a gift to unfold.

You can write to Christy at P.O. Box 448, Eastlake, CO 80614.

For Janet Tanke, editor extraordinaire, for support and encouragement. I'm lucky to have you.

And to the BICC—I wonder how I ever wrote without your support!

Also for Pam, friend, talented writer and confidante. Thanks.

One

"**A**re you pregnant?"

Lilly Baldwin's head jerked up and she met the icy fire in Nick Andrews's gaze. She dropped the pink carnation she'd been trimming as the door slammed behind him and more than six feet of pure masculine energy consumed her.

Nick stalked across the flower shop's wooden floor, his boots thundering, matching the slash of lightning etched between his dark-brown brows.

"I asked you a question," he said, slamming a copy of the *Courier* on the counter.

She looked down, seeing Miss Starr's gossip column.

Lilly's thoughts somersaulted when her doctor's name jumped out, along with the words, *relationship,* and *Kurt and Jessie Majors's recent nuptials.* It all but named Lilly as the small Colorado town's newest expectant mother.

Gulping, Lilly realized she had no choice but to brave

out the storm. After escaping the relationship with Aaron, she had sworn never to be intimidated by a man again.

She held her shoulders back courageously. "Yes," she said. "I'm pregnant."

He leaned closer. Even though she didn't want to, she took a reluctant step backward, away from the counter.

"Who's the father?" he asked with whiplash quiet.

Drawing a fortifying breath, she met his flashing blue eyes and softly confessed, "I haven't been with anyone… other than you."

Nick's quick curse made her wince.

"When were you planning to tell me?" he demanded, his words hammered together with rusty nails. "When you were showing? When Miss Starr ran a birth announcement this Christmas and I did the math? When I saw you in town with my child? When someone noticed a resemblance between me and my child? Never? When, Lilly?"

"I…" She discarded a hundred different answers, finally settling for the truth. "I wasn't planning to ask for your help. I know I'm capable of raising a child alone. I make enough money to support us both. I figured you didn't need to be burdened by this."

Instead of his fury diminishing, it flared. "You figured I didn't need to be burdened?"

"I'm the one who's pregnant," she supplied breathlessly, trying to make her explanation seem rational. "I'll take responsibility for the baby."

"Oh, you will, will you?" Lightning dug deeper into the groove etched between his brows.

"I didn't think the pregnancy would matter to you."

"You didn't think it would matter that I'm going to be a father?"

He'd whispered, sending a shock wave through her. After licking her lip, she said, "That night—"

"That night we made love? The night you shattered in my arms, calling out my name?" he interrupted ruthlessly. "The night you told me you couldn't get pregnant?"

She wrapped her arms protectively around herself. "I thought I was infertile."

"So how the hell does a woman who's infertile get pregnant?"

"I don't know." She shook her head, hardly able to believe it herself. "I'm as surprised as you are."

"I'll bet." His gaze swept down her body and paused at her midsection.

He'd done that before, she remembered, before he'd tugged down on her zipper, gliding his fingers across the agonizingly sensitized skin.

With a slow and gentle touch that melted away apprehension left from her previous relationship, Nick had undressed her. In spite of the reasons she'd had not to trust any man, her body had responded instantly.

Hot color chased up her cheeks. She didn't want to remember the level of vulnerability he'd exposed in her—not now, not ever again. "Please, Nick, you've got to listen to me. I tried for years to get pregnant. I even went to the doctor, and he ran some tests."

Nick said nothing.

After several seconds of silence, she sighed. "You don't believe me."

"Not a word."

"Surely you don't think I tricked you?"

"Why would I think that? Because you disappeared after spending one night with me? Because you lied about your ability to conceive, *even when I asked you if we should use birth control?* Because you kept the fact you're carrying my child a secret?

"Why on earth would I think you tried to trick me, Lilly?"

"You don't understand," she said, shaking her head. "I thought it would be easier on you this way, since you obviously don't want to be a father."

"What in God's name gave you that idea?"

"The way you kicked your family out of your life."

An ominous tick thumped in his temple. "What did you just say?"

Too late, she saw her mistake. Desperately she wished she could take back her thoughtless words.

"I asked you a question."

Having come this far, she had no choice but to push forward, fighting her own flight instinct. "It's not a secret."

"Then share it."

She should never have trespassed in his past.

"Share it, Lilly," he repeated.

"I heard—" She fidgeted, rubbing her shoulders, hoping to diminish the tension. Instead, it grew and stretched. "I heard that you threw Marcy and Shanna out of the house, leaving them homeless, when Marcy and you had a little argument. I thought since you kicked out one child that my having your baby wouldn't matter to you."

In his deep blue eyes, she saw the heat of temper switch to the coldness of rage. His hands bunched into fists, and she took another reluctant step backward. She should have shut up, she told herself, shouldn't have confronted him with the truth. Now it was too late.

The night she'd slept with him, she'd realized that he was twice the man Aaron was and three times as dangerous. That was why she'd run from Nick in the first place, leaving while he showered.

"You don't know a thing about my marriage to Marcy,

don't know a thing about my feelings for Shanna. You don't know a damn thing about any of it.

"But I will tell you one thing, Lilly Baldwin, *this* is about us—you, me, our baby—and the years that we'll be together."

Her knees threatened to buckle.

The need for self-preservation clawed at her. When she'd escaped Aaron, she'd sworn she'd never let a man dictate to her again.

But this man...this potent and threatening man...overwhelmed her. "I can see you're upset—"

"No. Upset was when you ran out on me the morning after we made love, without giving me the courtesy of an explanation. This—" he pounded a fist on the newspaper column "—is fury."

Swiftly he rounded the counter, pinning her against the wall, hands on either side of her head, his body only inches from her much, much smaller one.

She gulped, swallowing a lungful of air that sizzled with the electricity of his awesome anger. When he spoke, heat washed over her face.

"I had the right to know you were pregnant before I found out in the newspaper. I have the right to be in on all the decisions that affect my child and his future." His tone turned dangerous. "As of this moment, I claim my rights."

A surge of protectiveness rushed through her. This was *her* baby they were talking about. *Her* baby—the child she'd wanted her whole life, the miracle she believed she'd never experience.

"You were wrong, Lilly, about everything. Dead wrong."

"Be reasonable, Nick." Taking a deep breath, she tried to make him see things her way. "You've already got your own life, your ranch, and there's no reason for you to change anything. I don't need you to. I don't *want* you to.''

"You think I care what *you* want, Lilly?'' Carefully he enunciated, "I care about what's right, nothing else.''

Impossibly he stole even more of her space, along with the air she needed to breathe. In his eyes, spikes of blue blazed, a huge contrast to the desire she'd seen in their depths the night they'd first made love.

"If you wanted to play your games by your rules, you should have slept with a man who wouldn't care he was being used, a man who wouldn't care if you had his child without telling him, a man family didn't matter to. But you didn't. You slept with me.''

She shivered, but didn't know if it was from fear or a remembrance of their unplanned night of passion. How could she have given in to her own overwhelming need for him? How could she not have seen that his baby would matter to him? How could she have forgotten everything she'd learned about this man?

"Okay, Nick,'' she said, threading her fingers through her hair, then dropping her hand. "I didn't use you, but I understand how you feel, and I apologize.''

"It's not accepted.''

She fought for a calm she didn't feel. "We're both adults. I'm sure we can work something out.''

"Damn straight we will.''

His denim-covered thighs were pressed against hers, his masculine power threatening to consume her, like it had when she'd at once lost herself and rediscovered her feminine nature. With a sigh of frustration, she asked, "What do you want from me?''

"Marriage.''

Never.

Her shoulders sagged, and he curved his hands around them. At his touch, heat flashed through her, coiling in the pit of her stomach. She fought the temptation to give in to him again. She'd barely survived an awful marriage, and she couldn't give herself ever again to a man who had so much power over her.

"We made a baby, we'll provide him with a family and legitimacy."

"I can't marry you!" She defiantly looked him in the eye, in spite of the terror flashing through her. Wedding vows meant a life sentence, a ring exchanged for your freedom.

Lilly surged against his hands, fighting to get away, but his grip only tightened. "I'm willing to work with you. I'll give you visitation rights. The baby will know its father."

"Marriage or nothing," he corrected. "Within the next two weeks, before you're showing. Our child has already been the speculation of Miss Starr's column. I won't have him or her be the talk of the town, along with his mother." *Like Nick himself, like his own mother had been.*

To him, this issue was nonnegotiable.

Lilly carried his child. She would be his bride. And his baby would share his name.

They'd be together on holidays and birthdays, like a real family was. Nick would be there on Christmas morning.... Maybe because he had so few memories of his own Christmases, that thought made him pulse with pleasure.

Yeah, he'd be there to see presents being unwrapped, and he'd be there for every event of his son or daughter's life—school events, dental appointments, *everything.* Just the way it should be.

Marcy had robbed him of parenthood once; he wouldn't allow it to happen again.

Simple as that.

The fact that Lilly was every bit as manipulative as Marcy had been was immaterial. No child of his would be a bastard, wear that label and be whispered about. Not in Nick's lifetime.

"We don't know anything about each other," she protested.

"We'll learn."

Reaching up, she grabbed his wrists and tried to push him away. In her eyes he saw panic. A softer part of him wanted to give in, assure her that everything would be okay, that he wasn't the ogre she imagined. He'd battled her apprehension of men, of him, on their night together. And he'd won. But he didn't dare do it again.

She was no different than any other woman.

Two months ago, she'd made her bed and invited him to lie in it. He intended to do just that.

"You don't even like me," she said.

"Doesn't matter."

Her eyes squeezed shut and her breaths came in ragged little bursts. "It matters to *me*."

"There was a night we got along," he said, remembering her sensual response and the slide of silk as he'd slipped her clothing from her skin.

He'd held her breasts in his hands, felt their fullness and their response as her nipples beaded, begging for his touch. Even now, his body reacted just to the recollection of her tiny moans. "We liked each other just fine then."

"Don't remind me."

Oh, but he wanted to. He'd been good enough for her that night, if not now.

"You've got to see that this is insane."

"You've got to see that it's not." His grip tightened once again on her shoulders. "What kind of mother would subject her child to being a bastard?"

"A bastard?" she repeated incredulously. "This is a new millennium, Nick."

"Not here." Even when he'd been young, when plenty of single women had been having children, he'd been taunted.

"You're being old-fashioned."

"You're naive," he countered. "This is a small town and people will talk. Think about it." Nick had spent his childhood fighting the label of not being wanted, getting into more trouble than he knew what to do with.

His mother had been called down to the principal's office as many times as Nick had. By the time he finally finished school, he'd been suspended three dozen times. He wouldn't have been held up to scorn or ridicule if he'd had a father.

"It's more complicated than that.... I can't get married again."

"Why not?"

Her green eyes clouded. She opened her mouth to answer him, then closed it again. She had secrets, he saw, and he wanted every one of them uncovered.

"I just can't."

"Not good enough—not good enough for me, not good enough for the baby we made."

He didn't like the idea of being shackled any better than Lilly did. He'd sworn he'd never let another woman manipulate him again, but he was prepared to make sacrifices for his own flesh and blood. If he had to, he'd see to it that Lilly did the same.

He wound his fingers in her hair, then said, "This isn't about you and me anymore."

Her green eyes were wide, expressive, appealing. It had been her eyes that first captivated him, making him want to know her better. They'd laughed when she did, then later, they'd darkened with a desire that matched his.

"I've already promised that I won't shut you out. Isn't that good enough?"

"No." He shook his head. "Every kid deserves a father, no matter how you feel about the man you slept with."

She exhaled. "You're impossible."

"Maybe." Despite the accusations Lilly had flung like daggers to his heart, he had loved baby Shanna with his soul, which was still shattered from losing her.

The loss of one child who meant the world to him deepened his resolve not to lose another, especially one that was truly part of him. "But I'm willing to let you set the date."

"You can't make me marry you."

Uncurling one hand, he captured her chin, stroking the tender skin, his thumb grazing the column of her throat and resting where her pulse fluttered. "Would it be so bad?" he asked quietly, wonderingly.

She trembled beneath his touch, just as she had once before, igniting a passion in him that he'd been unprepared for.

At Kurt and Jessie's wedding, he'd asked Lilly to dance, and at first she had refused. He'd turned on his best smile, talked quietly and nonthreateningly, slowly changing her mind. They'd shared a dance, then a second.

Her responses had been seductively innocent and incredibly honest. Or so they'd seemed.

In reality, she'd been neither, playing him for a bigger fool than Marcy ever had.

He'd had relationships since his marriage was torn into jagged strips, but he hadn't allowed himself to be suckered.

Lilly had thrown a lasso around him and dragged him into her deceitful game, betraying him. He'd vowed never to be a pawn again, and that's exactly what she'd made him.

Her games were over now.

"Lilly, Lilly." He continued his gentle stroking of her throat. "I'd like to haul your pretty little butt down to the courthouse right now. Letting you set the date is being a whole lot more generous than I'm feeling." Abruptly he stopped caressing her. "Want to push me?"

She didn't respond.

"So how about it? What kind of ceremony should we have? A big one or a small, intimate one? And when should we do it? The choice is yours."

Tears shimmered on her long eyelashes, but he didn't relent.

His moral code didn't allow him to back down from what was important. And nothing in his entire life had been more important than this. Quite simply, family was family.

He took care of what was his.

No matter the cost.

"Choice?" she echoed. "What kind of choice is that?"

"The only one you're going to get."

She shook her head firmly. "I'm sorry, Nick. I won't marry you."

He moved his hand, clamping it on her shoulder. "Fine."

She expelled her breath in a relieved rush.

"Then I'll see you in court," he said.

"In court?"

"I'll sue you for full custody."

"No," she whispered desperately, trying to push him away.

He didn't budge.

''Please...'' Tears clogged her voice, her body went rigid and her knees threatened to buckle. ''You can't be serious.''

''Try me.''

Two

Lilly tried to dislodge the lump clogging her throat. With the set of his jaw, the ticking in his temple, the look in his eyes, Nick dared her.

"You'd really put our child through all that?" she asked, shocked.

"I'm doing the right thing. And the right thing is for our child to have both parents in his life and for us to be married."

"Then—"

"Barring that, unless you marry me, I'll do everything in my power to raise the child myself."

"You're trying to run my life."

"No, Lilly. As I've said, this is not just about us."

Her mind swam as she struggled to sort through the implications. He *would* sue. And with the legal system, he stood a chance of winning at least partial custody.

The idea of their child spending half its time with her,

the other half with Nick, made her shudder. She had divorced friends, knew of the struggles they faced. There would be Christmas holidays spent apart, sad goodbyes on Friday nights, birthdays and summer vacations to divide between parents....

And there was the fact the child would be illegitimate. She told Nick it didn't matter, wanted to pretend he was wrong, but he wasn't.

Columbine Crossing *was* a small town, and while most people would be supportive of her and the child, some wouldn't. Then there were the school years. Kids could be cruel, she knew. Like they had been to Nick.

But what of the cost to her?

It had taken a long time for her to gather the courage to leave Aaron and his constant criticisms. It had taken even longer for her to discover herself again, longer still for her to respect herself.

Until this instant, she thought she'd succeeded.

Nick's brazen scent, of mountains, man and determination, invaded her senses. His touch made her throb. He was too close, too overwhelming, and she was losing everything she thought she'd found....

Fighting a wave of dizziness, she let go of Nick's wrists, only to grab for a handful of his navy cotton T-shirt.

"Lilly?" he asked, his voice hollow, as if it came from a hundred miles away.

He'd stolen her choices.

He was dictating to her, controlling her life. He held the power, and she was left with nothing.

Damn it, damn him.

A second wave of dizziness made her knees buckle.

"Lilly! Answer me."

She fought against the threat of darkness, unable to think of anything except the baby growing in her womb.

In a move so quick she barely saw it, Nick caught her, sweeping her off her feet and cradling her in his arms.

Stars circled in front of her eyes, and her head rolled against his broad chest.

He held her gently, but firmly, and she knew she was safe.

This was the Nick she remembered from their night together, caring and courteous, not the man demanding her total surrender.

"I'm okay," she mumbled, struggling back from the edge of dizziness.

"Is your sister in the back room?"

"It's her day off."

He strode around the counter and toward the front door.

"Where are you taking me?"

"To the doctor."

Lilly grabbed hold of his shirt for stability, unnerved by the feel of him beneath the soft fabric.

Never slowing, he flipped over the Open sign to Closed and carried Lilly to his pickup truck.

For once she didn't mind him making her decisions. The dizziness frightened her, and she knew it scared him, too. Strength resided in that thought, wrapping her in security.

He gently slid her onto the bench seat, then reached around her for the safety belt.

His arm brushed the tip of her responsive breasts, and she gasped.

"Sorry," he said.

"It's okay, I'm just..."

He froze. His gaze sought hers. "Just?"

"Sensitive." Embarrassment clawed at her. With him she couldn't help but remember how she'd given herself so completely to him.

His glance took in her breasts, and she felt them fill, aching with something she hoped wasn't need....

Her hands shaking, she grabbed the safety belt from him and fastened it herself.

After climbing in beside her, he accelerated toward Third Street. With each minute that passed, she felt better. By the time they reached the doctor's office, there were no traces of dizziness or blurred vision.

Her assurances that she was okay didn't stop Nick from focusing his considerable attention on her. Even when she insisted she could walk, he carried her.

The nurse held open the door to an examining room, and Nick strode through.

"You can't come back here with me," Lilly protested.

He ignored her.

In the examination room, the nurse checked Lilly's blood pressure and temperature, then smiled.

"Is everything okay?" Nick asked. "The baby, Lilly..."

"Is he always this way?" the woman asked.

"Sometimes he's worse," Lilly replied, as a hot flush crept up her neck.

"You'll have to check with the doctor," the nurse told him. "But I can tell you that her blood pressure's normal and so is her temperature. You can rest easy, Daddy."

The door shut behind the woman, and Nick's gaze locked with Lilly's.

Daddy.

And in that instant, she saw Nick's point, very clearly. She didn't have a right to deny him anything, despite her fear, despite her hesitation. He'd shared in the creation of life, just as she had.

Where that left her, she had no idea. If he'd just be more willing to compromise, less rigid, less demanding....

But as he prowled the small confines of the room, wearing nervous energy like an aura, she realized he was none of those things.

Seconds later, the doctor knocked, then entered. "Lilly," he said in greeting. "Heard you've been seeing stars."

She drew comfort from the doctor's easy manner, knowing that if anything were seriously wrong, he wouldn't seem so relaxed. She closed her eyes in silent thanks.

"Nick Andrews," the doctor said. "Haven't seen you here since we took care of your mother."

"Lilly and the baby—they're both going to be okay?"

"That would make you…"

"Lilly's fiancé."

Her heart leaped as Nick's gaze connected with hers.

"And my baby's father."

"Ah," the doctor said. "Congratulations are in order, on both counts."

Nick stood so close to her, she could feel his heat. Out of the corner of her eyes, she could see him, arms folded across his chest, watching as the doctor checked her over. She tried to look away—anywhere but at the man who was the center of all of this.

"You didn't fall?"

"No. Nick caught me."

"And I always will," Nick said softly.

"Good, good."

A few seconds later, the doctor adjusted the stethoscope. "Well, young lady, it appears you fainted."

"What caused it?" Nick demanded.

"Any number of things—lack of regular meals, standing up too quickly, the stress of pregnancy on the body." Addressing Lilly, he added, "You'll be fine, but a little extra rest over the next couple of days couldn't hurt you."

Relieved, she nodded.

"Is there someone who can stay with you?"

"I will," Nick volunteered.

"Good, good. As soon as you feel up to it, you can resume all your normal activities, including sexual relations."

Butterflies fluttered deep inside her, knowing just what that meant. From the expression in his eyes, Nick remembered, too.

"I'll see you in a couple of weeks, Lilly, unless you have problems or questions, in which case, call me right away."

"We will," Nick promised.

Too late, she wondered if there was an inoculation she could have taken to protect herself from Nick and the effect he'd had on her one moonlit night, when she'd been swept away by magic and romance, and by the look of adoration a newlywed Jessie had for her husband....

Until that night, Lilly had never known a loneliness so painful it made her heart ache. Others had partners to dance with, husbands and boyfriends to love and hold. She'd had no one. Until Nick.

That one night had been like no other. She wasn't a woman who looked for pleasure anywhere she could find it. The way she'd been swept away had been completely out of character for her.

Then again, Nick Andrews wasn't like any other man she'd ever met.

She'd been standing by the punch bowl, feeling very much alone, when Nick had approached her. Befitting the best man, he'd been dressed in a tuxedo and was wearing a sinfully sexy smile. When he'd asked her to dance, her resistance had scattered.

Instinctively she'd known he was too devastating, too

dangerous for her. Trying to keep herself distant—and safe—she'd politely declined his first offer. But Nick had been persistent. Then before she realized it was happening, she'd been lost.

The doctor left, and reality returned with a resounding thud.

"Ready to go?"

"Really, Nick, I appreciate your thoughtfulness—" She nearly choked on the words, but she knew she had a better chance of getting her way if she didn't argue. "But Beth can stay with me." Her older sister would love the opportunity to fuss and nurture, Lilly knew.

And the thought of Beth caring for her wasn't nearly as unnerving as the idea of Nick making himself comfortable in her house....

"I'm sure she can," he agreed.

With gratitude, she felt the stress seep from her shoulders.

"But I'm going to."

"I don't want to argue," she said.

"So don't."

"Nick—"

"I'm taking care of the woman who carries my child. End of discussion."

She sighed in deep frustration, but she didn't argue further. To tell the truth, she'd been frightened silly and welcomed someone taking care of her. But darn it, why did he have to be so sexy?

"You want to walk, or do you want me to carry you?"

He offered his hand, and she reluctantly allowed him to help her down from the table. "I can walk," she said, pulling away.

That didn't stop him from cupping his hand possessively

around her elbow. *And they weren't even officially engaged yet.*

Outside, in the dappled warmth of the early summer sunshine, goose bumps chased up and down her arms—not from the breeze off Eagle's Peak, which stirred the tops of blue spruce and ponderosa pine, but from the way his touch made memory spark and flare.

She'd run away from him the morning after they'd been intimate.

In the harsh glare of morning sunlight, she'd seen her mistake for just that. Noticing that she was awake, Nick had eased her against him, his fingers tangling in her mussed hair. Softly and with a sexy drawl, he'd said they were good together, that he wanted to know her better. He'd asked her to start dating him.

Even then, she'd seen how powerful he was. Muttering an excuse to hold him off, she'd prayed he'd shower soon. When he had, she'd fled. The certainty that she wouldn't survive a relationship with him had clawed at her.

Now a relationship was exactly what she had.

He closed the pickup's door, then climbed in beside her. Thankfully, this time he didn't try to help with the seat belt.

Now that some of her worry had passed and Nick was no longer overwhelming her, she became aware of him as the man she'd met at Kurt and Jessie's wedding, the man who'd held her close and swept her off her feet.

She inhaled the hint of spice and sweat, the same scent that had wrapped around her when he danced with her.

Instead of turning west toward the town's residential area, where she lived, he headed east. Her heart sank and thoughts of their night together fled. Facing him, she demanded to know, "Where are we going?"

For a second, he took his eyes from the road. "Home."

"Home?"

"My home," he clarified. "The ranch. It'll be easier for me to take care of you at my place."

He was a whirlwind, and she was sucked up in it, in him. "Nick, this…you…you can't do this."

He directed his gaze back to the road, as if the conversation were over. "You heard what the doctor said."

"Don't twist his meaning to suit your wants."

"You shouldn't be getting stressed."

"So stop stressing me," she challenged, looking at the rugged planes of his profile.

He drove down the dirt driveway, parking in front of the ranch house.

Cutting off the engine, he turned slightly to face her, stretching his arm across the back of the seat, his fingers barely a half inch from her shoulder.

"Lilly, the doctor wants someone to stay with you. I'm your fiancé, you're carrying my baby. I'm the logical one to take care of you. I want to take care of you."

"I'm used to taking care of myself."

"I know." He gently touched her shoulder. "But you don't have to be tough all the time."

"I'm not."

"Then let me help."

Even through her lightweight sweater, she felt his warmth. And in his eyes, she saw that this wasn't a demand, it was a request. He knew how to cut through her defenses, she realized. "Nick, I can manage."

"You ran away from me that morning."

"Don't."

"You enjoyed our night together."

She couldn't respond, not with the way her heart was racing and the way memory warmed her insides.

"Didn't you?"

Heat flooded through her and seeped into her face. "It doesn't matter."

"It matters," he countered.

Blindly she scooted closer to the door, only to have Nick slide his hand behind her neck, his thumb gliding across the spot in her throat where her pounding pulse betrayed the emotions she wanted—needed—to hide from him.

"Was it just my imagination that you responded to me and fell apart in my arms?"

"Nick, stop. That night is over. It was a mistake."

He kept up the slow, maddening motions.

"Did I give you the same kind of pleasure that I received, Lilly?"

"You…"

"Did I make you feel things, make your body ache with need?"

"Nick, please. Do we have to discuss this?"

"Your response wasn't part of your lie, was it? A way to keep me interested and get me to lose myself deep inside you more than once?"

Heaven save her from him, his knowing touch, his sensual questions.

"Was it, Lilly?"

He wouldn't be satisfied until she answered, but could she? Where was the courage to admit something she'd rather keep secret? She had to be honest; he'd be on the lookout for anything less. "It wasn't a lie," she confessed, her voice shaky. "I…"

"Yes?"

"I wanted you."

"It's human nature for men and women to need each other."

"Maybe human nature," she said. "Not mine."

"Give in," he urged.

As she had before? She couldn't.

"Let me take care of you. Get the rest you need, take advantage of the fact I'll be at your beck and call."

"Nick…" She squeezed her eyes closed. Somehow, that only made the stroke of his roughened hands against her smoother skin feel like a contrast of satin and spurs. Each sensation seemed heightened and she wanted to respond.

She pried her eyelids open. Not missing anything—the parting of her lips, the change in her breathing—Nick watched her.

"If you won't do it for me, for you, do it for our baby."

He'd pushed her to the edge.

"How about it?" he asked, his strength enveloping her. "For now, give in."

Her pulse thumped and the air shimmered with danger. In order to appease him, she reluctantly conceded. "Temporarily. I'll stay with you temporarily."

He smiled then. Strangely, it wasn't triumphant. Instead, it made the darkness of his blue eyes a shade lighter, a shade less hostile and wary. She'd seen that expression before, the moment he'd feathered a thumb across her lip during their second dance at Kurt and Jessie's wedding….

After he released her, she all but shoved the door open.

Outside, air swept down from the fourteen-thousand-foot tip of Eagle's Peak, chilling where his touch had warmed.

"Cold?"

Didn't he miss anything? Shaking her head, she said, "I'm fine." Physically.

He draped an arm around her and drew her closer to him. As if they were really a couple…

A fresh shiver traced her spine. This time it was more than just the wind at work. If he had his way, they *would* be a couple, their agreement signed in front of witnesses. He'd have this kind of control over her all the time.

Once they were inside, he sealed the door shut. Possibility of escape vanished, and she felt her heart thunder.

Thankfully, he slipped his arm from her shoulder and moved deeper into the house. He left her alone, momentarily, in the foyer.

Lilly couldn't help remembering the only other time she'd been inside his home. It had been late, dark, and her attention had been focused solely on him. When he'd drawn her up the staircase, she'd only had time to notice small details about the master bedroom. The bed, framed in sturdy pine, was a study of masculine dominance.

Realizing he'd returned, she shook her head to dispel the image, then followed him.

"I'll light a fire in the living room."

"That's not—"

"Necessary, yeah, I know."

That didn't dissuade him. With a little tremor, she wondered if anything did.

He made her comfortable on the couch, pulling her legs onto the cushions and draping a cotton throw over her. Then he placed kindling in the grate, adding wood and sparking a flame. She watched him, mesmerized as much now as she had been two months ago.

His frame, as broad and rugged as the mountain peaks surrounding the town, stretched against the cotton material of his navy T-shirt. Equally dark denim jeans encased his legs and conformed to the slim planes of his hips.

She tipped back her head.

She knew all too well that under the jeans he was as solid and capable as he appeared.

What, she wondered for the hundredth time, had a single slip cost her? If she'd had any idea her future would be entwined with a man this overwhelming, she would have stayed home from the wedding and sent Kurt and Jessie a gift.

Placing his hands on his thighs, he pushed himself upright.

She was attracted to Nick, and that's why she'd surrendered herself to him. Now, desperately, she wished she weren't so incredibly aware of him.

He reached over and tucked a strand of hair behind her ear. It was a small act, easy and so very intimate. It made her heart miss a beat.

"Do you need to call Beth?" he asked.

"Oh, no!" Her hand went to her throat. In her hurry and worry, she'd forgotten to let her sister know the store wasn't covered.

"I'll get you the cordless phone."

He did. But he didn't give her any privacy. Instead, he stood near the fireplace, arm stretched across the mantel as he listened to her explain where she was and that she wouldn't be at work tomorrow.

"Is he refusing to marry you?" Beth demanded once she was certain Lilly was fine. "If he is, I can come over there myself and give him a piece of my mind."

Lilly turned her gaze away from him. "No."

"Then that means he asked you to marry him? I told you he would, once he knew about the baby. Oh, Lil, this is fabulous! Just fabulous!"

Lilly didn't agree.

"When's the wedding? Can I be your maid of honor and should I let Mom and Dad know that you're getting married, after all? They'll want to hear it from you, but since you're going to be at Nick's for a while, I'll—naturally, we'll do the flowers," Beth gushed, tripping over herself in her excitement. "How about some red tulips in the bouquet? It'd make a splash."

"Red tulips?"

"Red ones...you know, as a declaration of love."

Her heart twisted.

Beth rushed on. "Did you set a date yet? And have you given any thought as to how we'll all spend the holidays? Oh, Lilly, this is just too exciting."

Lilly took a breath. Against her will, her gaze was drawn back to Nick. He was studying her carefully, the same way he had when he'd carefully lowered himself on top of her—

She nearly dropped the phone.

Nick reacted in an instant, moving across the room and taking the receiver from her. He explained to Beth that Lilly needed rest, promised they'd be in touch, then hung up.

"Did she upset you?"

Lilly shook her head, but he frowned, crouching next to her and placing his palm across her forehead. The contrast of him—strong, and work-roughened hands against her much smaller body, heat melting chill, masculine against feminine—made her insides warm.

Nick paused, capturing her gaze. "I'm sorry," he said softly. "Finding out about your pregnancy...our baby... I should have handled it better." He feathered his fingers into her hair, smoothing the layered strands back from her face.

"You're sorry?" she managed, her heart thumping.

"For upsetting you."

Her heart tightened. She thought, hoped, for just a second, that he'd back down, agree to a compromise. But the words *compromise* and *Nick* didn't fit in the same sentence.

"If anything had happened to you or our baby..." He trailed off, then swore softly. "I would never forgive myself."

His gut-honest words, husky with remorse, weakened a part of her she was trying to steel against him.

This was how it had started with him, she knew, exactly how it had happened that night. He'd hidden nothing from her, telling her how he was reacting to her, sharing feelings Aaron had always shut her out of.

Nick had asked the same in return, not allowing her to hide. He'd encouraged her to let go, and with his gentle encouragement, she'd behaved in ways she'd never imagined possible.

Now he was doing the same thing again, exposing his emotions and disarming her at the same time. It was working. Even though she knew better, she was responding with womanly warmth.

"I won't push you, Lilly." He continued in that same honest way that made rational thought impossible. "But I'd like for us to be married in the next couple of weeks. I want you under my roof, where I can protect you, take care of you, make sure you get what you need.

"I know you don't want it, but it's the right thing for our child. I think you know that."

He was right. She couldn't do to her child what had been done to Nick. Even though he hadn't told her a lot about his past, she'd heard the hurt in his voice when he talked of being unwanted.

Lilly couldn't, wouldn't do that to their baby.

She didn't know what had happened between him and Marcy. But the tightening of his lips when Lilly had repeated the rumor that he kicked out his wife and baby told her the gossip had been wrong.

He would love their baby, even if he'd never love Lilly. He had a right to be a father. Gently he drew her hands between his, as if saying she held his life in her hands.

Their gazes met and held, and she couldn't think.

"Lilly," he said, his voice husky, "this time I'm asking, for all our sakes, will you marry me?"

Three

He tried not to squeeze her hands too tightly as he waited for her answer. To Nick, nothing had ever been more important than this moment.

If she forced the issue, he'd see her in court, just as he'd promised. But he didn't want that for his child; he wanted a two-parent family.

And he wanted Lilly as his wife.

The horror that had rushed through him when she'd pitched forward had paralyzed him. His movements had seemed to be in slow motion as icy fingers scraped his spine. He couldn't move fast enough, wouldn't be able to catch her, wouldn't be able to save her, *wouldn't be able to save his child....*

He'd lost one child. He'd crumble if he lost another. That meant he needed to take care of Lilly.

Earlier, he'd seen that the strength she projected hid an air of vulnerability. Whether she realized it or not, Lilly needed someone to look out for her. She needed someone by her side to slay her dragons.

She needed him…just as surely as he wanted her.

In his nearly thirty years, he had never met a more stubborn, aggravating female. The fact that she appealed to every one of his senses only made her effect on him all the more irritating. He was all too aware of her, femininity and desirability in an intriguing package that his fingers itched to open.

Damn it all.

"Say yes, Lilly," he urged, patience evaporating.

"I…"

He waited.

She worked on her lower lip, causing it to swell and making him ache to caress it and soothe away every one of her hurts.

Fact was, he wanted to do that with every aspect of her life, had since he'd first taken her in his arms and held her against his chest at the wedding reception.

She'd resisted at first, pulling away when his palm found her bare back, then jumping when he rested his fingers in that curve at the base of her spine. He'd leaned down, whispering in her ear, swearing he wouldn't do anything she didn't want him to do.

It hadn't been until their second dance that she'd relaxed at all.

He'd been attracted to her, even when her eyes had spoken of hurt. But by the time they'd stopped for punch and carried their glasses outside to the patio, something inside him had shifted.

When he'd talked, she'd tilted her head to one side, actually listening to what he said. Instead of planning what she'd say next or trying to be witty, she'd given him her full attention. There'd been no pretenses.

He'd noticed the way her lips parted invitingly when she smiled. He'd seen her as an attractive woman, no doubt, but she'd stirred something more, something deeper inside him.

During their third dance, when she laughed at one of his ridiculous jokes, he realized he wanted to know her better and that his desire went beyond a physical need.

That same mix of emotions existed now.

He continued to regard her, watching her reactions, noting the way her light-brown brows drew together in confusion, then eased into something he hoped was resignation.

"You're right," she said after a long, weary sigh. "But only because it's the best thing for our child…"

His heart jumped out of rhythm.

"Yes, Nick. I'll marry you."

He squeezed her hands tightly. "Soon."

"Nick…"

"One day our kid will be able to do math and figure out how long we've been married."

"You don't give up, do you?"

"Not when something matters."

She closed her eyes, tipping her chin heavenward, as if seeking strength.

"This matters," he added. "You matter."

She looked at him.

"We'll make it work," he promised. Somehow. It wouldn't be a real marriage, not like his first one had started out—until Marcy had taught him a few lessons in deceit and pain.

He knew up front that Lilly wasn't any more honest than his first wife had been, but at least this time, he wouldn't be a fool. This wasn't about love, it was about responsibility. Simply, it was a business arrangement for his child's sake. Nick never intended to forget that, no matter how tempting his new wife could be.

When Lilly smothered a yawn, guilt hit him. He was supposed to be taking care of her. "You need to rest," he said.

"I feel fine, honestly."

"I don't," he confessed. Releasing her, he strode to the window, then turned back to face her. "You scared the hell out of me."

"Yes," she whispered. "It scared me, too."

Somewhere deep inside, in the heart he'd thought couldn't be touched again, Nick felt a stirring. "You'll tell me," he asked, "about the pregnancy, everything the doctor said?" He wanted to share the details, every aspect of the new life growing inside her. Marcy had denied him the right to know anything. She hadn't even wanted him in the delivery room. Of course, now he knew why. That right had belonged to another man.

With this child, he was being given a second chance at fatherhood. Nick Andrews might have been many things, but he wasn't stupid. He'd learned not to pass up opportunities.

It had been a second chance that turned his life around, saving him from the destruction he had recklessly been charging toward. He'd been seventeen and had made the mistake of being home when his mother's latest lover had staggered from the bedroom at noon, naked and hungover, scratching his chest and demanding to know what the hell Nick wanted.

Nick's mother hadn't tried to stop him from leaving, even when she'd seen him fighting tears.

Angry at her, her latest live-in and the world, Nick had driven around aimlessly before ending up at Kurt Majors's house.

Ray and Alice Majors, true to their reputation of being caring people, had opened their home and their hearts to the unwanted teen.

They'd taken Nick in, given him a place to stay, taught him about respect, caring and friendship. They'd shown him how to ranch, made him do a fair share of the work and chores, just as they had with another of Kurt's friends, Shane Masters. For the first time, Nick had felt as if he belonged. Most of all, though, the Majorses insisted he finish high school, even though he hadn't cared.

That May, at the small graduation ceremony, his mother hadn't sat in the bleachers. Kurt's mother had, though, and she'd cheered for him.

Now he was being given another chance to be a daddy. He'd be damned if he'd blow it.

"I'll tell you, Nick. I promise not to keep anything else about our child from you."

In thanks, he bowed his head.

"So far, everything's been perfect."

He looked at her to see her smile, a feminine, serene smile that walloped him in the solar plexus. He'd never seen such uninhibited joy before.

"Our son or daughter is due around Christmas. The doctor said babies come at their own time."

Nick actually grinned. The timing couldn't be better. He'd have a wife, a baby, a Christmas tree, brightly wrapped presents for both beneath the branches....

He'd have the opportunity to be part of his child's life from the very beginning. He'd be in the delivery room, and he'd receive the greatest gift of his lifetime.

It was perfect, simply perfect.

"You heard Dr. Johnson—I don't have to go back for another visit for a couple of weeks."

"I want to go with you."

Her smile didn't fade. "I figured as much."

He scored the victory of her capitulation, realizing she truly didn't intend to shut him out, even if their marriage would be against her will.

He couldn't help himself. He smiled back. Nick realized he got further with her—like he did with the fillies on his ranch—when he took things slowly, not insisting on having his own way. It was a good lesson, one he'd be wise to heed.

Being patient didn't come easily. But for the sake of his family, he'd try.

"I bought a book of baby names," Lilly admitted.

"And?"

"I was wondering if you had any favorites."

As long as the child shared his surname, Nick didn't mind. "Whatever you want is fine with me."

"What?" she asked, her mouth widening with mock shock.

He liked her this way, he decided. Her green eyes had lightened by several shades. Her defenses were down, taking his along with them. This was the woman he'd held, the woman who'd swayed against him. "I don't have to have everything my own way," he said, then added, "just most things."

Her smile widened and his blood surged and skipped. It made him wonder how different things might have been if she hadn't run away from him, if she hadn't betrayed him with secrets, if she didn't despise the idea of becoming his wife.

She stifled a second yawn. "I kept you up longer than I intended," Nick said.

Lilly's glance flickered to the floor above them. "Where will I sleep?"

"Where do you want to sleep?"

She released her breath in a rush.

"Uh…do you have a guest room?"

What had he expected? They'd shared a bed once, but she was obviously in no hurry to do so again.

He told himself it didn't matter. His body sent another message, though, one that was as difficult to ignore as the feminine scent of her.

"Yeah, I have a guest room."

While the seconds dragged by, she said nothing.

Even though he knew he'd regret it later, he gave in to the demand gnawing its way through his insides. Moving across the room, he dropped to his knees near her and took her delicate hands in his.

Their gazes met, and for a moment he saw beyond the distance and dishonesty back to the night they'd trusted each other completely. He softened toward her. After smoothing her hair back from her face, he said, "I'll show you upstairs."

"I remember the way."

He remembered showing her….

Standing, he pulled her to her feet, until their bodies all but touched.

Her breaths came closer together. So did his. He wanted to be immune, but wasn't.

Instead of releasing her completely, he moved one hand to her spine, finding the hollow and resting his fingers there while he walked upstairs beside her.

She didn't pull away, a minor victory.

On the landing, she reached for the nearest doorknob. "This room okay?" she asked.

"No," he said, covering her hand before she could open the door.

"I thought that one was yours," she said, looking over her shoulder.

"It is."

"Then...?"

"Your room is next to mine."

She frowned in confusion. "What's wrong with this one?"

Instinctively he tightened his fingers on hers. "This one is private."

So private even he hadn't been inside for three years.

The door to Shanna's nursery had remained closed, and he'd forbidden anyone to enter, including the housekeeper. "There's no bed in there."

"Then—"

"Leave it, Lilly." He knew he was being unreasonable, but that didn't change facts. "Your bedroom's over there."

She nodded, but before she entered her room, she glanced back at him.

Their gazes locked, then without saying a word, she went inside, shutting him out.

He turned to head downstairs, not sure how he was going to dispel the energy churning inside him.

He paused at the closed nursery door, running his fingers over the metal knob. Cold, burning cold, stung his palm.

His jaw set, he strode down the stairs, his boots echoing with a lonely, empty sound.

Lilly moved to the window, staring at the vastness of the high mountain prairie. Cattle grazed in the distance, and a few determined trees reached toward the sky. Everywhere there were wide-open spaces, nowhere to run, nowhere to hide.

She folded her arms protectively.

The house rang with silence, unlike the way it had sounded when she'd previously spent the night here. Then it had been filled with quiet kisses and satisfied sighs.

Now the air was thick with tension. What had gotten into him, she wondered, when she'd almost entered the wrong room?

Downstairs, when he'd wrapped her hands in his, she'd look into his eyes and had seen hope. In an instant, all that had changed. Despite the summer sun streaming through the window, she shivered.

She had no choice but to marry the man, share her life with him. It would come at a huge personal cost to herself.

Marrying him was the right thing to do, she knew. The only thing to do.

So why was doing the right thing so scary?

Lilly saw Nick stride toward the stables, then lost sight of him. She tried to rest, but couldn't even sit still…not now that her world had been dumped upside down, making her question if she'd ever be the same.

Silence oppressed her, and she couldn't stay in the room another minute. Deciding to find something to drink, she headed toward the kitchen, only to pause outside the door he'd told her was off-limits.

She shouldn't invade his privacy. But if she was going to be his wife, sharing her life with him, sharing this house with him…

Squaring her shoulders, she went downstairs and filled a glass with water. She took a deep drink, noticing that her hand shook.

Pacing, she wondered when Nick would be back, wondered what secrets he hid behind a closed door.

Five minutes later, she gave up the internal fight. Climbing the stairs, she turned the knob he didn't want her to touch.

Her heart thrummed.

Rusty hinges groaned before reluctantly opening. Then the air vanished from her lungs.

A crib nestled against one wall, and a fluffy comforter was draped over the wooden side, as if waiting for a tiny body to snuggle under it. A stuffed pink turtle rested beside a small pillow, and a mobile dancing with cartoon characters hung from the ceiling.

Despite herself, Lilly was drawn into the room, her footsteps muffled on the thick, rich carpeting.

A rocking chair sat in the middle of the room, next to a table with an abandoned pacifier.

She covered her middle with one palm, then, with her free hand, picked up the book lying on the table, its spine broken and pages yellowing. *How To Be a Great Daddy* the title read.

Tears sprang to her eyes.

In that instant, she knew....

Nick had said she didn't know a thing about his marriage, didn't know a thing about his feelings for Shanna.

He was right.

The gossips had been wrong...she'd been wrong.

Nick had loved his child; he wouldn't have kicked out his wife and baby. And now he'd be doubly determined to be part of this child's life. He deserved that chance.

"I'd forgotten I bought that."

She jumped, the book crashing to the floor. Guiltily she spun around to face him, her skirt swishing around her ankles.

He stood in the doorway—filled the doorway—one shoulder resting against the jamb. His straw cowboy hat dangled from his index finger and his sweat-dampened T-shirt clung to the width of his chest.

"Nick, I..." She trailed off, pressing her hand more firmly against her middle.

He shook his head.

"I'm sorry." She blushed.

"You have the right," he said. "It'll be your house, too. Guess it was inevitable you'd come in here." Lines were sharply grooved between his brows, but resignation was the only thing in his deep blue, unreadable eyes.

"Haven't been in here for three years." Pushing away from the wooden casing, he moved toward her.

Stopping only a few inches away, he tossed his Stetson on the table and stooped to pick up the fallen book. His frown deepened. *"How To Be a Great Daddy,"* he read.

"You were never given that chance."

"No."

She reached for him, curling her hand around his wrist. His head snapped up and his gaze burned into her.

She felt his heat, his strength, the differences in their sizes. "Why didn't you stop the gossips?"

Lilly saw the tiny throb in his temple.

"They were wrong, weren't they?" she persisted. "You didn't throw Marcy out of your home."

"Yes," he corrected. "I did."

Lilly pulled away her hand. It was back, the iciness that frosted his blue eyes.

"Packed her bag and heaved it down the stairs."

Hearing the coldness in his voice, she swallowed.

"The rumors were right, Lilly. Don't fool yourself. I fought her every step of the way in court, too, fought for custody. Ended up giving the lawyer more money than I gave her. Nearly bankrupted me."

He hadn't released her gaze, and she saw the pain in his eyes.

"And I'd do it all again."

Defiantly meeting his gaze, she said, "There's more to it."

"Is there?"

The book still lay in his hand, telling her so much about him. "You cared about Shanna."

"Loved her. Only time in my life I've ever unconditionally loved anyone."

The only time? Even though things had been beyond horrible with Aaron, she'd grown up wrapped in her family's love. "Then you wouldn't have thrown her and Marcy out without good cause."

"Are you sure?"

She'd seen him fight already, had seen his concern for her. She wasn't foolish; she knew he was worried about their child's well-being, but he had been about Shanna's, too. "Yes."

"Like maybe the fact Marcy was having an affair?"

Lilly squeezed her eyes against nausea.

"She didn't come home one night. I told her to move out, that marriage meant people were honest, that they didn't run around or lie to each other.

"She broke down and sobbed, telling me she was pregnant."

Of course Nick took her back. His moral code wouldn't permit him to refuse. "So…?"

"Everything was fine, till David Sampson showed up, wanting his girlfriend and his baby."

Lilly couldn't breathe.

"Shanna wasn't my baby."

"She lied…?" Lilly whispered.

Nick nodded. "And the damnedest thing?"

The emptiness in the soft-spoken words made her heart twist.

"I told Marcy it didn't matter. Told her I'd keep quiet. No one would ever have to know she was a tramp. I would have forgiven her anything as long as she didn't take my baby away from me. No one would ever have known

Shanna wasn't my flesh and blood. Didn't matter to me.'' He paused for a second. "I loved her like she was my own. That was the only thing that mattered.

"I begged, Lilly, begged her not to destroy me and tear apart our family. I begged her to let Shanna know me as her daddy, give her a chance for an intact family.''

"Like you never had.''

"Like I never had.''

Pain for him filled her heart. Marcy had betrayed him, then had taken his ideals, his emotions, his love for a child and stomped on them.

And now that Lilly had tried to keep her pregnancy secret from him, he'd believe she was no better than Marcy. Their marriage didn't have a chance. *She* didn't have a chance.

"When she laughed in my face, refusing and saying she was in love with David, that she wanted to be with him, that I would never see Shanna again, I threw her out, just like the gossips said.''

"That's only part of the story, Nick.''

"Is it, Lilly? Is it?''

"You were within your rights to act that way. You didn't throw an innocent woman and baby into the street. No one can blame you for what you did.''

But the bleakness in his eyes said he blamed himself more than anyone else ever would.

"I wondered…what I could have done differently. Should I have worked less hours, not worked as hard to buy land and the cattle to graze on it? Should I have questioned her when she said she was going to get a cappuccino with her friends? Should I have demanded she be home by a certain time, so that she was in bed when I was?''

"You did everything you could. Don't blame yourself.''

His lip curled.

She knew, all too well, how easy it was to accept the blame rather than place it where it belonged. But maybe... maybe together they could learn to heal.

"I'll love our child with my heart and soul," he swore, reaching out to enclose her in his arms.

"I know."

Slowly he moved one hand up, his knuckles sliding up the column of her neck, the curve of her cheek, then grazing her ear. Opening his hand, he cradled her head.

"As my wife, you'll have my protection."

She didn't know whether his promise comforted her or frightened her.

His fingers feathered through her hair. She knew she should resist, pull away. Yet somehow, she couldn't. Nick wove a spell over her, just as surely as he had the night of Kurt and Jessie's wedding.

"Don't do this to me, Nick," she pleaded, even as her eyes drifted shut and she gave in to the power of his caress.

His thumb massaged her nape, easing the worry that had settled there.

"Don't do what?" he asked. "This?"

He deepened the pressure and her head drooped forward. Even with her eyes closed, he overwhelmed her senses. He smelled potent, of man and desire.

"Or this?"

His other hand joined the first, working magic on the knots in her shoulders. Absently she wondered if he'd drawn out her common sense along with the tension.

Her forehead rested on him, and she reached a hand out to support herself, finding a fistful of cotton.

At the feel of rough chest hair beneath the shirt, she froze.

She was close, so very close, to surrendering to him once more.

"Or maybe this?" he asked, sliding one hand down her spine.

Lilly pushed away from him, linking her hands together to resist temptation.

To her, he was more dangerous than a flash flood, sweeping her legs from beneath her and taking the ground along with it.

She'd never had a man affect her this way, she realized, sucking in breaths, one shallow inhalation at a time. He made her forget everything—that he didn't trust her, thought she was no better than Marcy; that he didn't want her, just the baby.

Lilly didn't dare forget, not ever again.

He was consuming.

And he was going to kiss her.

To save herself, she hurried to the sanctuary of her bedroom, slamming the door and sliding the lock in place.

Leaning against the door, she shook her head.

She'd been right earlier. She shouldn't have entered the nursery, unleashing a torrent of sympathy for him that made sanity drift away like a hawk riding a Rocky Mountain thermal.

He had the power to run her life, and he'd use it. That much he'd made clear.

She reached to smooth back her hair, realizing her hand still shook. His scent still lingered on her clothes. Branding her as his? she desperately wondered.

Nick's footfall sounded in the hallway, loud like crashing timber.

Then suddenly, silence reigned.

Her head drooped forward. He'd stopped in front of her door. In rushing out of the nursery, she'd gotten a reprieve, but it wouldn't last.

When he knocked, she jumped.

Like a coward, she didn't answer.

"When we're married, there won't be any closed doors between us."

She shivered, but not from his threat. Rather, from the terrifying realization that part of her didn't want doors closed between them, either....

Four

Needing an outlet for the energy churning inside him, Nick prowled the kitchen.

Yesterday his life had been perfectly ordered. Marcy's betrayal and the loss of Shanna had been locked in memory, the key thrown away. Today, every recollection had been unearthed and exposed by his future wife.

He grabbed a beer can from the refrigerator.

His future wife.

If he had his way, they'd be married in less than two weeks—not bad for a man who'd sworn he'd never again wear a woman's lying promise on his ring finger.

The can opened with a satisfying hiss.

Even if love wasn't an option, he intended—in every other way—for them to be a married couple. He'd share everything with her—his home, his life, his bed....

Nick took care of the things that were his—especially his family. Lilly's needs were secondary.

He drank from the can, long and deep.

Who the hell did he think he was fooling?

It mattered what Lilly wanted, mattered a great deal. She was going to be the mother of his child. Despite his threats, he knew she held power.

Yet he was learning the way to get past Lilly's defenses—gentle words and a gentler touch. He'd discovered that when they'd danced, talked, made love....

Lilly was a wonderful woman, one who thought with her heart more than her head. After Marcy, that was a welcome change.

The thought of Marcy brought his anger back to the surface. The two women were nothing alike. He knew that, but he'd still been furious when he discovered Lilly had never intended to tell him about his baby. Even though he'd locked his emotions off from all women, his heart had stopped when she nearly fainted.

Nick crushed the can in one hand.

He cared about her. He didn't love her, wasn't capable of that, but yeah, it mattered what she wanted.

She was getting to him.

In less than a couple of hours, she'd tested his physical resolve, making him hungry for her. And she'd pushed him to the edge emotionally. She'd probed his past, entering Shanna's room against his wishes and asking questions about Marcy.

Then Lilly had had the nerve to close a door in his face.

She had guts.

He'd meant it when he said there would be no closed doors between them after they were married. He was every bit as attracted to her now as he had been two months ago. She stirred something inside, and a part of him realized that it went deeper than wanting to be part of his child's life.

Even though he refused to love again, they would live together as husband and wife—in every sense.

Their future would be anything but boring, he knew. He figured it was a good thing he didn't much care for boring.

Dragging his emotions—and hormones—under control, he took a couple of steaks from the freezer to thaw, then headed outside to complete his chores.

He'd stormed out of the ranch house this morning before his work was done. Getting the truth out of Lilly had been more important than anything else and had crushed every other thought. Seemed she had a habit of doing that to him.

The screen door slammed behind him and Nick knew he needed physical release. Exercise was better than nothing. Being away from Lilly and the scent of her lingering in the air wouldn't hurt, either.

Lilly was too restless to take a nap, and she couldn't stay locked in her room all day, even though instinct urged her to do exactly that. So where had that instinct for self-preservation been two months ago? she wondered. If it had been stronger, she wouldn't have succumbed to Nick's power.

But then, she wouldn't have a baby growing inside her, the child she'd wanted, prayed for.

She only wished there was a way to have the baby without being tied to Nick.

Sounds of him moving around drifted up the stairs, along with the scents of steaks grilling. Her stomach grumbled; it had been hours since she'd eaten. Even if she preferred to avoid Nick, she needed to keep her strength up.

Knowing she was beaten, she ran a hand across her hair, hoping to finger comb the tangles from it. She smoothed her broomstick skirt and summer-weight sweater, then realized she was stalling.

Determinedly she made her way to the kitchen, another room she hadn't seen on her previous visit.

Hearing her nearly soundless footsteps, he slowly turned, and the sight of him overwhelmed her.

She'd forgotten just how handsome he was.

When he smiled, his eyes lit with pleasure, chasing shadows from the deep blue and making them shine. A small cleft split his chin, tempting her to rest a finger there.

He'd washed up since he'd been outside, and a new T-shirt was tucked into black denim jeans. He smelled fresh and clean, and seemed so accessible.

Warning bells tinkled in her mind again. This was Nick at his best. She knew there were other sides.

"How're you feeling?"

His rich voice slid over her, like a silky rose petal rubbed against bare skin.

When she didn't answer, he closed the distance in a few strides, resting his powerful hands on her. With him so close, she could barely think. "I'm fine."

He lifted one hand to feel her forehead.

"Honest," she said.

His knuckle gently grazed her cheekbone. "You're still pale."

"Because you didn't give me a chance to get my makeup before you did the caveman routine and dragged me out here."

"You are feeling better," he teased.

She was melting inside. His touch, his tone...

Instead of dropping his hand, he placed his thumb at the corner of her mouth.

She fought the temptation to turn toward his palm and allow him to cradle her head.

If she wasn't careful, she might allow herself to forget that he was no different than any other man, that he'd decided what was right in her life and given her little say in the matter.

She'd fallen for him and his sensual approach once before; she couldn't allow it a second time. She only wished that determination alone would bring her pulse rate back to normal.

Reaching up, she grasped his wrist, trying to move him away, but the attempt backfired.

With her hand still wrapped around him, he traced a finger downward, over her chin, the column of her throat and the small hollow there. He stopped just beneath, at the same place her breath felt frozen.

Lilly, desperate for air, told herself he wouldn't touch her any more intimately, that he wouldn't wander farther downward, to cup her breast in his palm…like he had once before.

She had hold of his hand, and she had the power to stop him at any time. She *would* stop him, she told herself, proving she was strong and determined.

Still barely breathing, she looked up at him, her eyes seeking reassurance in the deep, deep blue of his.

She found anything *but* reassurance.

"Tell me it didn't matter to you."

Mesmerized by the shadows clouding his eyes, she could only swallow.

"Tell me that it was just a one-night stand, that you never thought about us.…"

She was powerless to resist when he did exactly what she'd thought he'd might.

She felt the friction of his callused fingers against her lightweight sweater, saw how dark his sun-bronzed skin looked next to the creamy color of the fabric, and she shuddered at her own reawakening.

"...Tell me that you never wondered how it might have been if you hadn't run away. Tell me, Lilly."

"I can't..." *Can't talk, can't breathe, can't think...*

"Ah, so you did wonder. Just like I did."

He'd wondered? Did that mean he'd thought about her, too—that to him it was more than just a one-night stand? She'd known he wanted answers as to why she ran, but she'd convinced herself she meant nothing to him, except for the tiny detail of her having his baby.

"Tell me about that," he encouraged. "Tell me what you wondered."

His palm curved as he continued to move his hand down the middle of her chest. Her gaze was riveted on him, and she was captivated by his strength, the force of his will.

When she didn't answer, he said, "I wondered. A lot. I got out of the shower that morning, ready for you, even though I was trying not to be." His voice sounded scratchy, as if he needed to clear his throat. "I turned off the hot water, Lilly, because I wanted to be able to restrain myself when I came back to bed."

She tried to take a step backward, only to have him tighten his grip on her.

"It didn't work. Even the towel dragging on my wet skin reminded me of the way you reached for me, the way you wrapped your hand around me. Were you serious when you said you'd never done that for another man?"

Heaven save her, she wanted the floor to open and swallow her whole. That night she'd done a lot of things she'd never done before.

"Were you, Lilly?"

"Yes," she finally managed to admit.

Nick moved. Despite her mind's protests, she did nothing to stop him. She cried out when he cradled her breast in his palm, testing its weight.

Unable to help herself, she hung on to his leather belt, not wanting to let go. The same feelings had engulfed her that starry night two months ago.

It had been the desperation to hold and be held that had frightened her the most.

With his encouraging words and sensual suggestions, Nick had proven he was far more dangerous than Aaron had ever been.

"Your breast feels fuller than it did before," Nick said, leaning forward to whisper the comment in her ear. "Does it to you?"

He wouldn't allow her to hide.

"Does it, Lilly?"

"Yes," she gasped when he closed his hand.

"And what about your nipples?"

Her eyes closed. She was drowning in her own response.

The end of his thumbnail trailed across her nipple. Need, raw and aching, filled her. Her knees gave out, and he was there, moving to support her.

She gave thanks she was still fully dressed; otherwise she doubted she would be able to take any more.

Part of her wanted to push him away, make him stop. But the same renegade part that had once accepted his invitation urged her forward.

He dragged his nail across the sensitized tip once again.

"Our lovemaking meant something to you, Lilly, didn't it?"

"Yes."

"Is that why you ran?"

He hadn't stopped caressing her. She would have been angry with him if she could have thought straight, but he didn't allow that.

"Were you scared?"

With that question, he stilled his hand.

Slowly, so very slowly, she opened her eyes and looked at him. She couldn't find her tongue, and it was suddenly difficult to form words. Finally she admitted, "Terrified."

"Why?"

The confession came slowly. "You made me feel things I've never felt before, convinced me to do things that I never dreamed possible. You scared me."

"Was it me you were afraid of?" he asked. "Or was it yourself?"

"Both," she whispered.

"You should have told me."

"Would you have listened?"

"Listened, yes."

"It wouldn't have mattered to you that I was scared, would it, Nick?" She fought to find common sense, reminding herself of the feelings he'd aroused in her, recalling the reasons she'd run in the first place. "You would have said we could work it out, work through it."

By small measures, he released her, until they stood near each other, close but not touching.

She hugged herself.

"We could have," he said.

Lilly knew she'd been right to run.

"But you never gave me that chance," he said.

"Because you would have stolen mine."

He raked his fingers through his dark hair. The wind had already blown through it, and now it looked wild, untamed.

"I couldn't let that happen, Nick."

"Doesn't matter, because now we're together."

Her stomach tightened.

"Is it so bad?" he asked. Silently he reached a finger up to tuck a strand of hair behind her ear.

Even the gentlest of touches made her yearn for more. What happened to her when he was near? Even her husband hadn't aroused this kind of response from her, and at one time she'd believed herself to be in love with him.

"Is it?" Nick asked again, his eyes holding hers prisoner.

"How would you like it if the tables were turned?" she countered.

"They're not."

"That's not my point," she protested.

"If you were to drag me into your house and keep me there, saying we would live together as man and wife…" he said. "I wouldn't mind."

"You're twisting my words."

Tension scattered with his lopsided grin. "Yeah."

Her eyebrows drew together. She'd seen a lot of sides to Nick—seductive, intense, angry, determined—but this smile, his teasing after being so serious and sensual, surprised her, making her realize she knew almost nothing about him.

And they were going to be joined together to raise a child.

The thought was dizzying, like being on a carnival ride, suspended upside down.

Nick looked toward the door. "I think the steaks are ready. Are you hungry?"

"Ravenous. Seems to be a constant feeling."

"You going to eat me out of house and home?"

"You're the one who insisted on bringing me here," she said, then smiled.

"And I'm not sorry. Steaks should be about done."

If a carnation suddenly sprouted roselike thorns, he couldn't have kept her more off balance.

While he served the steaks, Lilly found her way around the oversize kitchen, taking out silverware and glasses. She had little choice but to learn her way around this place.

Somehow, she doubted he'd go for the idea of her living in her own house after they exchanged vows.

Their bodies accidentally brushed more than once, sending little pleasures cascading through her. She didn't want to be aroused by him, but just as surely, she was.

"Shall we toast our upcoming wedding with ice water?" he asked once they were seated at the table. "I'd offer you wine, but it's not good for the baby."

Or for her, for that matter. Maybe if she hadn't sipped champagne at Kurt and Jessie's wedding, Nick wouldn't be proposing a toast now.

"To us," he said, lifting his water glass in Lilly's direction. "And a successful marriage, baby and all."

His gaze captured hers, and she couldn't look away.

Throughout dinner, Nick kept the conversation light, telling her about his ranch and the cattle he ran on its one-hundred-twenty acres.

Then tension ratcheted up another notch when he told her of his plans to hire additional ranch help so that he'd be around more to help take care of her and their child.

"That's not necessary, Nick. Really."

"I've made my decision."

"Your decision?" she asked. "What about my decisions?"

"Like?" His fork clattered against the stoneware plate.

"Like the fact I'm going to continue working, even after the baby is born. If we need to, we can hire a nanny."

"There won't be any nannies, Lilly. Our baby will have a mother and father. That's all he'll need."

"There you go again," she protested. "Making plans in my life."

"Our lives," he countered.

"Fine. Our lives. *Our* lives. Both of us get to make decisions."

"Don't get upset," he said, reaching to cover her hand with his. "It's not good for you."

Electricity jolted through her at his touch, and she pulled her hand away and dropped it into her lap. "Easy for you to say. As long as we do everything your way there's nothing to get upset about."

"Lilly, I know how to compromise."

She challenged his lie. "Then we'll hire a nanny."

"Why would we need to when I'm here?"

"*You're* going to take care of the baby while I work?"

"Something wrong with me fulfilling my fatherly obligations?"

The idea of him—all six feet of masculine power and energy—holding a tiny child, changing diapers, feeding it and offering comfort, pacing the floor and rocking it to sleep, filled her with tiny thrills.

She tried to imagine what their child might look like. Would their baby have a shock of dark hair, like Nick? And would blue eyes peer at her with the same kind of intensity that was reflected in the depths of Nick's enigmatic gaze? Or maybe her eye color would prevail and she'd see a reflection of herself in her child's face.

But the image that excited her the most was the idea of Nick peering downward into trusting innocence. He'd be an excellent father; she had no doubt of that. Nick excelled at everything he set his mind to. And he'd set his mind on her and their unborn infant.

"Lilly, I've told you I'm not an ogre."

It would be easier if he were, if she could dislike him.

"Rest while I clean up here."

"I don't want to rest."

"Doctor's orders."

"*Your* orders."

"My orders," he agreed, with a sheepish smile.

She opened her mouth to protest, then closed it when she realized if she was in the front room, at least she'd be away from him.

Lilly made her escape. Sitting in the living room, on the large, bulky leather furniture that screamed "male domain," she wished she could close out the sound of his humming. Men didn't hum. And men didn't do dishes. They especially didn't hum *while* they did dishes.

He was so irritating, frustrating, dictating, charming....

She buried her head in her hands.

A minute later, that's where he found her. "I'm okay," she said, heading off his concern, or so she thought.

He crouched in front of her, lifting her feet from the floor and shifting her until she lay on the couch. Then he reached for a woolen throw and covered her with it.

"How about a fire?" he offered.

"Don't you have chores?"

"Did them while you rested. I'm all yours."

Thankfully, he moved away, tossed a couple of logs on the grate, then struck a match, the crackle of the flame punctuating the awkward silence.

She didn't want to be captivated by him, didn't want to watch every one of his sure motions. And suddenly she didn't want to remember how wonderful it had felt to be held in his strong arms as he led her gracefully across the dance floor....

He pivoted and looked at her, one brow raised in question.

Lilly turned away.

Crossing to the stereo, Nick slid in a CD. One of the same songs they'd danced to at Kurt and Jessie's wedding floated through the air, a slow George Strait ballad that went straight to her heart.

She finally found the courage to glance at Nick again.

He gave her that crooked smile. "Dance?"

"You know I'm not a good dancer."

"You're an excellent dancer."

She frowned.

"At the wedding, Kurt told me I'd be missing out if I didn't ask you to dance."

Her frown faded. Aaron had told her she had two left feet, and she'd believed him.

"Come on, Lilly, what can it hurt? Unless you don't feel well—"

She knew—all too well—what it could hurt.

She could use the excuse that she needed to rest. But it wouldn't be the truth. In reality, a secret part of her—the wild and curious one that she thought she'd tamed—wanted to be in Nick's arms.

He extended his hand. She was lost.

His fingers wrapped around hers, and he drew her to her feet, continuing until she stood only inches from him.

"Put your arms around my neck."

She did, all but standing on her tiptoes. At least at the reception, she'd had on heels, making the eight-inch difference in their heights a little bit less intimidating. Now she was all too aware of how small she was compared to him.

"I won't bite," he promised, his palm at the small of her back, urging her closer.

She felt him, all of him, male and hard, pressed against her body.

At first she moved stiffly. Slowly, though, the combination of his gentle sway and the reassuring words of the song loosened her.

Logs in the fire sparked, and she didn't know if the warmth she felt came from it or from the way he held her.

The latter, she suspected, her breath squeezing out when one of his hands slid farther down her back.

Possessively he held her, encouraging her to move even closer.

Possessively?

That's what it was, no doubt. She'd sworn she'd never be a man's possession again. But pressed against him like this, magic happened....

She laid her head on his chest, surrendering.

"I could do this all night," he said softly.

The man was a master. When it suited him, he could reduce her to a puddle. He held her the right way, spoke in the right intimate tone, moved in perfect unison with her, making it seem as though she really could dance. He erased her thoughts of escape and replaced them with want. He'd done it to her once before, in exactly the same way.

She knew better, now, but it didn't matter.

"Penny for your thoughts."

Lilly didn't dare. "Inflation..."

"Okay, I'll up the ante. How about an entire night without me nagging you," he offered.

"Sold." With a smile, she tipped back her head to look at him. "I was thinking I shouldn't be doing this with you."

"Oh?"

"It's dangerous."

"Why?"

The very danger she spoke of flashed in his eyes. Brightened by firelight, his eyes seemed to stare into her, looking for her secrets.

"I know better. You seduced me—"

"Is that how you think it happened?"

Her steps faltered. Instantly he adjusted his until they once again moved in unison.

"I remember it differently," he said. "I remember seeing you standing by the punch bowl, all alone. And that dress…"

She'd bought it especially for the occasion, on a dare from her sister. Black, silk, form-fitting and open in the back, it was unlike anything Lilly had ever worn before.

"I wanted you out of it. But that wasn't why I asked you to dance. I wanted to see your eyes looking into mine."

Her eyes?

"I'd noticed your eyes, before. At the post office. You were delivering a bunch of flowers to the post mistress."

"Bouquet, Nick. Not a bunch of flowers, a bouquet."

"Bunch, bouquet, whatever."

"Pink carnations," she said. "That's what Bernadette likes. Traditionally, they mean I'll never forget you."

"Flowers mean something?"

"Yes."

"Tulips?" he asked.

He'd obviously remembered her conversation with her sister. "Yellow ones mean hopeless love."

"What about red ones?"

Reluctantly she answered, "They're a declaration of love."

"Your sister wanted them in your bridal arrangement?"

"She doesn't know the truth about our relationship."

"So what would you choose?"

"Nick—"

"You're the florist. You'll make our arrangement. Tell me what you'll choose."

"Stephanotis," she said.

"For?"

"Happiness in marriage. And violets."

"Violets?"

"Faithfulness. To prove I'm not your ex-wife."

He held her tighter, but said nothing.

They continued to move and sway against each other. A part of her wished the moment could last forever.

"Does Bernadette at the post office know about the carnations, what they mean?"

"Yes. She asked."

"She'll never forget someone?"

"I heard there was a man she was interested in, a long time ago."

"Funny. I just thought she was always this age, with no past."

"There's a lot we don't know about people, Nick."

"Yeah. Half the fun is the discovery."

She smiled, and when he rewarded her with one of his own, she forgot to move.

He stopped, too, and the music continued softly.

"Has anyone ever sent you one?"

"One what?"

"A bunch of flowers. Bouquet."

She shook her head.

"I'll have to take care of that."

With a small amount of pressure on her spine, he started to move again. Effortlessly she followed. If only their lives could be this easy. The problem was, in most areas of her life, she didn't want to fall in step with his lead.

"You'd brought Bernadette a book."

"She likes to read, as much as I do. Love stories with tragic endings—you know, like Romeo and Juliet." Why was she telling him all this?

"To go along with the pink carnations?"

"Yes."

"I'd noticed your eyes. You were holding the flowers near your face. Your eyes were sparkling with mischief.

But that disappeared when you saw me looking at you. It was like a shutter dropped over them, as if you were frightened to have me looking at you so deeply. Wasn't that right after you moved back to town, after your divorce?''

Her face drained. He knew a lot about her, she desperately realized.

''Sore subject?''

''It's in the past,'' she said.

''So why that same look now?''

''The same look?''

''Your brows are drawn together. Your eyelids are narrowed, and your eyes are a darker green than they were before. It's the look that says back off, the one you've used to keep half the male population in town from beating a path to your door.''

She tried to pull away, but he tightened his grip.

''I can tell when I'm too close, Lilly. You had that same expression on your face before I got in the shower that morning. Later I kicked myself for not reading you better. I won't make that mistake again. So tell me…why did you agree to come home with me?''

She knew he wasn't talking about this afternoon…and her heart hammered when she realized he'd held her tightly in his arms.

He'd wanted answers since the morning she'd walked away from him. Over the following weeks, he'd left half a dozen messages on her answering machine at home, had stopped by the flower shop twice. Fortunately she'd seen him coming and convinced her sister to lie to him, saying Lilly wasn't there. The time he'd come to her house, she'd pretended not to hear the doorbell.

''Hmm?''

He was right; he was too close. Men who got too close hurt her.

The ballad ended, but another began.

"I don't know," she confessed, unable to look away. She'd asked herself that a thousand times.

"You were lonely," he guessed.

"No...yes." At the wedding reception, she'd been thinking of all the people who were with their lovers, then thought of her big, empty bed.

"This morning, you said you were sure it was my baby, that you hadn't been with other men."

"No other man, ever, except my ex-husband."

"Ever?"

The single word sent a shiver down her spine, and so did the honesty he wanted.

"Ever."

"So why me?"

She laughed. "At the time, you seemed...safe."

He quirked a brow over his electric-blue eyes.

"I was a fool," Lilly said with a rueful smile.

"Were you?"

"I knew you didn't sleep around," she said matter-of-factly.

"I beg your pardon?"

Color rushed into her face, drowning her cheeks in embarrassment. "I'd heard that you weren't into casual relationships."

He said nothing.

"You didn't have a reputation." She wished the floor would open up.

"You'd asked?"

"I'd heard," she corrected. She didn't add that Bernadette Simpson at the post office had told her, before Kurt and Jessie's wedding, when Nick's name—as best man—came up in conversation. Bernadette had said some nice things about him, adding that she'd figured he'd only behaved badly after his divorce because he'd been backed into a corner.

Bernadette's words had swirled in Lilly's mind when Nick had come up to her at the reception. "And I figured if you were friends with Jessie and Kurt, you couldn't be too dangerous."

"So how about now?"

"Danger comes packaged a lot of different ways."

He looked at her deeply. "Did it work?" he asked quietly. "Us sleeping together—did it stop you being lonely?"

She couldn't look away from the sizzling intensity in his eyes, couldn't pull away from the hold he had on her spine, her nape, couldn't stop herself from answering honestly, "No. It didn't stop me from being lonely." In fact, it had only made the emptiness worse.

"Then maybe this will clear it away."

His grip tightened and he pulled her against him. Determinedly he lowered his head.

Her heart fell to her toes.

He was going to kiss her.

She knew it without a doubt.

Five

When he'd asked her to dance tonight, he hadn't intended to kiss her.

But now that she was in his arms, cradled against his body, he didn't intend to let her go without doing so.

A surge of possessiveness walloped him, unwelcome and unwanted.

It had taken him years to exorcize the scars Marcy left on his soul. And on the day he'd finally thrown their wedding pictures into the fire, he'd sworn he'd never again let a woman get close.

But now…

Now, he not only wanted Lilly close, he intended to keep her there.

He didn't like his own emotional response to her. That, however, didn't stop him from moving. Cupping her chin, he held her still for his kiss.

"Nick…"

He liked the way she said his name, with a tremor of desire that said she wanted his kiss, even if she fought that desire. "Yeah?"

"I…"

Before she closed her mouth, he caught her bottom lip between his teeth. He gently laved his tongue against the fullness of her lip, then suckled it.

She sighed. He half expected her to pull away, but she didn't.

"I'm going to kiss you, Lilly."

Her eyelids flickered, and he caught a glimpse of her green eyes, the color lightened—by expectation? he wondered.

Not letting go of her, he brushed his lips against hers, once, then twice, waiting for her surrender.

She didn't disappoint.

Slowly she opened her mouth for him.

As if he'd waited half a lifetime for this, he claimed what she offered.

Primal and primitive, need consumed him.

He deepened the kiss, his tongue seeking hers. With a tiny moan, she responded.

This hadn't been the way it happened the first time. Back then, she'd been unsure. But this Lilly was asking for something in return.

If he'd found her sexy before, he now found her undeniable. She swayed toward him, and he moved, placing one of his legs between hers for support.

Leaning into him, she took the initiative, and he felt her tongue against his, tasting, exploring. Her warmth washed over him, making him hard.

It was too soon, he knew.

He'd wanted to dance, nothing more. He'd wanted to

chase away her loneliness. He hadn't thought the same feeling would seep into his own soul.

Until this moment, he hadn't given loneliness a passing thought. But this afternoon, the house had no longer rung with hollowness. When he'd returned from his chores, he'd known she was inside, waiting for him. For the first time in years, Nick felt alive.

Before he lost all control, he ended the kiss. His heart hammered, like it had when he'd sneaked Susan Milden into the Majorses' barn.

Alive. Yeah, that was a good word for it.

"You're an excellent dancer, Lilly." He looked down into her eyes. They were barely open, but hazel spikes across the rich green reflected her inner thoughts. "Don't let anyone tell you otherwise."

Surprising him, she didn't immediately pull away. "This won't work," she warned.

"What won't?" He prayed she had no idea of the effect she had on him.

"This…"

"Go on."

"Kissing me won't convince me to let you run my life and make my decisions."

No, but it might scramble *his* brains. "That wasn't what I was doing," he stated.

The flare of desire faded into a frown of distrust. It was back, her wariness of him.

Reflexively his grip tightened. Drawing a breath, he forced himself to relax.

"So what were you doing?" she asked.

"Dancing with my future wife."

"Why?"

"Why?" he repeated.

She waited.

"Because I wanted to."

She laughed, a disbelieving little sound.

"Surely you can't think I'm not attracted to you?" He frowned. "I get it," he said. "You think I was touching you, kissing you because I want to manipulate you. So that you'll agree to my demands."

"That's what it seems like."

"Lilly," he said softly, very, very softly. "I don't know what your experience was with Aaron, but I don't manipulate the women I'm involved with. If I want something my way, I'll say so."

With his index finger, he brought her chin back around. "And when I kiss you, you can be damn sure it's because I want to, because I'm hot for you." He proved his point with another deep kiss, leaving them both out of breath.

"And unless you want me to take you upstairs to my bed and prove this is about sex, a pure physical attraction for you, I suggest you find your own room and lock the door."

With her shoulders squared, she turned on her heel and walked quickly up the stairs.

The slam of her door shook the landscape painting on the wall.

Nick paced the living room, emotional and physical energy churning in his gut. It was about desire, as he'd told her. But he hadn't been walloped with this kind of feeling in more years than he cared to count. There was something else. He wanted her to want him, like she had that night. *Like she'd never wanted another man.*

He wanted her, ring, marriage, baby and all.

The sooner the better.

It was going to be a long night, he knew, with temptation only one door down.

* * *

"An engagement ring?" Lilly asked, her fingers clamping around her cup of decaf.

"Women who are getting married usually wear one," Nick replied, leaning across the table toward her.

"But—"

"You said you were feeling well enough to go in to work," he countered.

"That's different," she protested. But she had a hard time trying to keep to her point. This morning, only inches away from her, across the kitchen table, Nick was doubly devastating.

He'd showered, and dampness still clung to the thick strands of his hair. A stray lock curved across his forehead, making him look even more appealing. He'd shaved, leaving the scent of soap and spice filling the air she breathed. He'd dressed in dark denim jeans that hugged his hips and ruggedly muscular thighs.

Worst of all, he'd left the top two buttons of his long-sleeved cotton shirt unbuttoned, giving her a glimpse of the darkly matted hair beneath.

She remembered running her fingers across his chest, his back and lower....

She gulped her coffee, then winced when the heat stung her mouth.

"So how's it different, Lilly? You're okay enough to go to work, but not shopping?" He shoved his coffee aside. "Are you running away, or is it my ring you don't want to wear?"

"No. Yes." Trapped by his insight she sighed. When she'd told him she was ready to go back to work, she'd been hoping to get away from him. She wanted to be alone to think. Even in her own room, his proximity had threatened to overwhelm her. Every time she fell asleep, she'd dreamed of him. She hadn't been able to get away....

"Yes?" he prompted.

"I thought I'd just wear a simple band."

"I'm a traditional sort of guy. Humor me."

As if she had a choice.

"If he's available, we can talk to Matt Sheffield while we're in town. See when he can perform the ceremony."

She squeezed her eyes shut against the surge of emotion. Nick was moving too fast, like a tornado devouring the prairie.

"Unless you prefer to be married by a judge?"

Stunned, she looked at him. "You're asking my opinion?"

He expelled a breath, then covered one of her hands with his. "I've told you I'm not an ogre. This is as much your wedding as it is mine. Work with me, Lilly."

His honesty rocked her. When he was demanding, she could ignore him. But when he exposed his emotions, she could deny him nothing. "Being married by a judge seems less hypocritical."

"There won't be anything hypocritical about a minister marrying us, Lilly. We will be living together as man and wife."

"But love won't be involved," she objected.

"No. And if it helps you, we can have the word left out of the vows."

Five years ago, in front of a minister, in a church filled with friends and family, she'd sworn she'd love Aaron. He'd given her a ring, but he hadn't meant a single word he'd said.

"I will honor you, Lilly Baldwin, even with the last breath in my body."

"What about trust?" she asked

He didn't answer.

Honor had to be enough, she knew. He'd offer nothing

more. Maybe he wasn't even capable of giving anything more. "If I wear a ring, it has to be a small one," she compromised.

"Fine."

It wasn't, though, she found out an hour later.

Since he'd taken her to his house after the doctor's visit yesterday, Nick's first stop was her home so she could pick up toiletries and clothes, then he'd driven straight to the town's most exclusive jeweler.

"Nick, you promised."

"Small is relative, Lilly."

"If you're Elizabeth Taylor."

He grinned.

Then, unnerving her, he zeroed in on the exact ring that attracted her eye. Signaling the shop owner, Nick said, "We'd like to see this one."

She grabbed his arm. "That's one of the biggest diamonds they have."

"Looks medium size to me," he said. "Isn't that right, Jed?"

"Been making rings most my life," Jed agreed, pulling a marquis-cut diamond from its velvet holder. "It's about medium size."

"Give me your hand, Lilly."

"Nick, I can't accept this ring." Yet even as she protested, the gem caught a ray of sunshine and refracted it in a hundred different directions.

"Can't hurt to try it on."

It fit. Darn it a hundred times. It fit perfectly, and it looked beautiful.

"Yes, sir," Jed said, rubbing his grizzled chin. "No doubt 'bout it. That's a mighty fine ring."

"Like it?" Nick asked her.

Her heart accelerated when she realized it was so much

more than a piece of jewelry; it was a symbol of her commitment to their temporary marriage. Suddenly it weighed a ton.

Nick took her hand in his palm and held the ring beneath the jeweler's lamp while Jed gave Nick all the information about the gem.

"Do you want to look at a different one?" Nick asked her.

"A smaller one," she said.

"It's as small as I'm going to buy."

"It costs too much."

"Nothing is too much for my future wife. And if you like it, I want you to have it."

In that instant, no one else existed. She looked at him and was stunned by the sincerity etched in the hardened angle of his jaw.

Aaron had wanted to possess her, but it was all about him, what she could do to make him happy. Right now, Nick seemed to want to make her happy.

"We can look at another one," he said.

She shook her head. She wanted—desperately—not to like the ring, but it was more breathtaking than anything she'd ever owned.

"We'll take it," he told Jed.

Breath squeezed from her lungs.

"Now, since it's part of a set, this wedding band goes with it," Jed said. "Want to try it all on together?"

"No," she told the man. For now, this was enough.

"Do you have matching bands for the groom?" Nick asked.

"Sure 'nough."

"You're going to wear a ring?"

"I'll be as married as you are, Lilly."

"But—"

"Lilly, a ring's part of my promise to you and our baby."

With a sigh of resignation, she agreed. With each step he took, he brought her closer to the inevitable.

Nick needed a size larger than the one in stock, and he wouldn't buy it unless Jed promised it would be ready in less than a week.

She doubted she'd ever known a man more demanding than her fiancé.

"Now, little lady, would you like to wear your ring?"

Before she could answer, Nick said, "We'll take it in a box."

While she worked the band from her finger, he told her, "I want to give it to you later, when we're alone."

Alone.

Her mind seized the single word and replayed it a hundred times. The thought of them alone again in his house gave her goose bumps.

"Hungry?" he asked when they were outside.

Summer's warmth washed over her, and for a few minutes, took her cares along with it. And the idea of being fed definitely appealed to her. It had been hours since breakfast.

"The Chuckwagon Diner's serving lunch."

"You know me," she said.

"Always hungry?"

She smiled up at him.

"Wish I had a camera. A smile like that's worth a man's soul."

He held open the door for her, and she wondered what it might be like if she believed in love, if he believed in love.

Her smile slowly faded. Happily ever afters might exist

for some people, she knew, but she definitely wasn't one of the lucky ones.

"Do you have a guest list?" Nick asked.

Lilly looked up from the magazine she was absently flipping through. She'd tried to read her new book about Antony and Cleopatra, but it hadn't held her interest. In desperation, she'd turned to a magazine, but hadn't had much better luck with it.

Surely there couldn't really be a hundred and fifty ways to improve her love life.... And even if there were, she wasn't interested.

Being imaginative in bed had caused this problem, and there were no columns that dealt with what to do after you'd had a fabulous night of passion. "A guest list?"

"For the wedding."

"Surely we won't be inviting that many people."

His shoulders filled the room's entryway. He blocked the early afternoon light, and she wished he'd stay there, but knew he wouldn't.

"I'd just like to invite my family," she said. "Maybe a few of your close friends."

"You don't want a big wedding?"

"No, I already had one. It wasn't what I'd hoped."

"Then a small wedding's fine."

"You're scaring me, Nick. It's not like you to be so agreeable."

"Just want you to set the date."

"You don't give up, do you?"

"Nah."

He grinned, and her heart forgot what it was supposed to do next.

"Next week?" he said.

"Two," she countered.

"Done."

She'd been had. The moment the word left her mouth, she'd known it.

"I'll call Matt and set it up. Morning or afternoon?"

In the morning, so that she had all day and night to get through with him? Or afternoon, where night nipped at its heels? He'd already promised there'd be no closed doors between them.... "You decide."

"Any place in particular for a honeymoon?"

"We've already had it."

He moved then. In three strides, the sound of his boots muffled by the carpeting, he approached near her, until she had to tip back her head in order to look at him.

He filled her vision, made her stomach warm and tight.

"We'll have our honeymoon, make no mistake about it."

She couldn't swallow.

"I expect my wife to sleep with me, and I mean that in all senses of the word. I'm just offering you the chance to get away for a few days, if you want."

The fire in the grate snapped and crackled.

"I..."

"I can make love to you as easily here as at a fancy hotel. It's up to you."

She didn't know what to say.

"I've been waiting all day for this," he said, his voice husky, like it was before he kissed her, made love to her.

Nick knelt on one knee before her.

This close, he was even more overpowering.

"Give me your hand, Lilly. I want to put my ring there. I want the world to know you're mine."

Her heart thundered.

Nick reached for her hand and held her wrist steady when it shook.

His head was bent. She closed her eyes, then wished she hadn't when she saw images of herself desperately yanking at Aaron's ring, trying to rid herself of his hold.

This wouldn't be the same, not at all. The world didn't have enough places for her to hide from Nick's determination.

The past and present merged, suffocating her. Lilly pulled her hand back, sending the ring bouncing to the carpet.

"Lilly?"

"I can't do this, Nick. I thought I could, but I can't."

"Okay, okay," he said, his voice low and soothing, a contradiction to anything she'd ever heard from him, except during lovemaking.

He gathered her against him.

He was the one man she shouldn't seek comfort from, and he was the only one she wanted.

As he stroked her, muttering meaningless words, her emotion slowly subsided.

When she hiccupped, he moved away, not stopping till he stood halfway across the room, near the fireplace.

She dragged in a few deep breaths, steadying her nerves.

He drummed a finger on top of a poker. Even from here, she saw the tension bunched in his shoulders.

"Help me out, Lilly," he said, stilling his hand. "I want to understand what's happening here." He dragged spread fingers through his hair.

It took a great deal of courage to look at him. He was more masculine than anyone Lilly had ever met. Bold. Daring. Compassionate. And darn it—her future husband.

"Why do I scare you?"

"You don't."

"But you don't want to make love."

"No," she admitted, facing him.

"You didn't like it?"

She had no choice but to confess the truth to him, as well as herself. Finally looking at him, she said, "That's not it."

"I could have sworn I satisfied you. That little gasp, the way you dug your heels into the mattress, then the way you collapsed beneath me..."

Something was happening inside her, an awareness.... A chord of recognition made her realize she was woman to his man, that they were meant for each other, no matter how she fought it. "I... you...yes, you did."

Never, in all her years of marriage, had Aaron asked these kind of questions. He'd never cared enough. "But it was the first time ever—" She broke off, knowing she'd said too much.

"You mean to tell me you were married and you'd never had an orgasm until we'd made love?"

When she didn't answer, he swore softly.

"What the hell kind of marriage did you have?"

"Not a good one," she admitted, trying to regain her emotional distance from him.

"I want to hear about it, Lilly. Every single detail."

Where he'd been understanding earlier, he was now radiating raw male determination.

"Neither one of us leaves this room until I know why the idea of being intimate with me again frightens the life out of you."

Six

Patience had never been a virtue Nick had much interest in developing.

Unfortunately, for as long as he was going to be involved with Lilly, he had no option but to try.

He just wished it wasn't so damned difficult.

He wanted to cross the room, take hold of her shoulders, hold her, kiss her…something, anything to melt that icy shell around her heart.

He ached for her, and he hadn't felt anything this deep and penetrating since he'd held baby Shanna in his arms for the first time.

"Lilly, I'm waiting," he said, tempering his words, even if that was one of the hardest things he'd ever done. "Why do you act like marrying me is a life sentence?"

"Because it is."

Her words echoed in the room and pounded in his heart. She saw this—him—as punishment for her sins.

"It's about control," she said. "I don't want to lose it again—I swore I never would. A wedding band is a shackle that will tie me to you, and I won't be able to get out."

Beneath his breath, he swore.

Before he thought of what to say next, she softly explained, "Everything you've guessed about my relationship with Aaron is right."

"Including the fact you didn't have a good sex life?"

"Sex was one of my responsibilities."

Nick's gut clenched. The idea of a woman making love with him out of a sense of obligation sat like a burr in his gut. "A responsibility?"

"Three times a week."

"He told you that?"

"All the time."

"Whether you wanted it or not?"

"That was irrelevant. Aaron needed the release to deal with his stress."

She blinked, then looked at Nick through the long veil of her light brown lashes, not hiding anything. She had the power to make him simultaneously want to protect and possess.

"After the first year, I didn't want it. Ever."

"So why did you stay married to him?"

"If I could have a dime for every time I've asked myself that question..." She attempted a smile that fell flat. "When I met him, I fell in love, head over heels. I wouldn't have married him unless I loved him.

"I was young, out on my own for the first time. I'd gone to Durango to attend college and Aaron had already graduated. He had a good job, his own apartment. I was flattered by his attention to me—a nobody from a small town."

"A nobody?" The words stuck in Nick's craw.

"That's what I thought."

"And Aaron reinforced that?"

"At first, no... He showered me with attention, took me to his apartment, encouraged me to fix meals, instead of us going out."

"He wanted you to take care of him."

"Yes. But I didn't see that then. He proposed, and I was swept off my feet. He was older—wiser, I thought—and I believed he wanted what was best for me. I only wanted the best for him.

"He had his own place. If I moved in with him instead of staying in a dorm, I could save my parents some money. We agreed that after I graduated, we could start a family. I wanted two kids—Aaron said that was fine with him."

This time, the tension in Nick's gut felt strung out, like razor-sharp barbed wire.

"I told you about my infertility, Nick. I didn't lie to you. I didn't trick you that night."

He drummed his index finger on the head of the poker, saying nothing. At this point, her words were irrelevant. She was carrying his baby. That was all that mattered.

"After I graduated, he convinced me that it was better to be a stay-at-home mom, that he earned enough money to support his family. I loved that idea—it was my picture of a perfect marriage and a perfect family. But pretty soon, he called me lazy."

Nick couldn't hold back his sneer. He knew how hard she and her sister worked to make Rocky Mountain Flowers a success—hours of sweat and toil every week.

"Three years later, I had no money, no checkbook, no baby...."

Protectively her hand covered her abdomen. He'd seen

her do that several times, and each time, something inside him lurched.

Marcy had done little but complain the whole time she'd been pregnant—she was losing her shape, feeling fat; the baby moved too much; she couldn't get comfortable.

But Lilly, with the way the baby mattered so much... He couldn't be sorry she carried his child, even if he still suspected she'd lied to him.

"I didn't even like trying to conceive, not after..."

Color drained from her face. He needed to stop this, now. "Lilly, don't."

"I'm okay," she said. "If we're going to... You have a right to know why I—why the idea of being married again scares me."

His hand gripped the poker.

"I went to the doctor. At first she told me to relax, that I was stressed out. I tried everything—taking my temperature, trying to get in the mood, wearing sexy negligees, but when he..." She took a breath, tipping up her chin to meet his gaze. "I didn't enjoy it. Aaron just got in bed, then got on top of me."

"Whether you were ready for him or not?"

Her gaze dropped.

Rage filled Nick. He slammed the poker against its metal holder. He thought of nothing except the churning urge to wrap his hands around the coward's neck and make the slimy bastard hurt the same way he'd hurt Lilly.

"After six months, I went back to the doctor and asked Aaron to do the same. They did all these tests. It was awful. But I would have done anything. We'd been married for two years and...nothing had happened.

"According to Aaron, the doctor said his sperm count was good—"

"Not good enough."

She shook her head. "And said it was a problem with me."

"That idiot husband lied to you."

"That's what Dr. Johnson believes must have happened. I'm sorry, Nick—I would never have made love to you if I'd known. I'm not the kind of woman who would do something like that. I know you don't believe me, but—"

He moved to her, placing his hand over her lips, sealing off the words. "It doesn't matter."

Her eyes were wide, telegraphing how important it was to her. And because it was, it had to matter to him. He'd been in a lot of difficult situations in his life—hell, they'd honed him into the man he was today.

But he knew—*he knew*—nothing had ever been as important as the next few minutes. Softly, he said, "I believe you."

She pushed his hand away. "You do?"

"Yeah. I do."

She leaned forward. "You're not just saying that?"

"I mean what I say, Lilly. You should know that."

"I know."

Her sigh did more to his insides than any lovemaking ever had. He captured a lock of her hair and twirled it around one of his fingers, liking the way the strands felt, like the slide of silk.

"You don't know what your belief means to me, Nick."

"Yeah, maybe I do." He saw it in her eyes. Her integrity was important to her. To him, as well.

"Thank you," she said.

For a moment, he wondered how he'd ever doubted her.

"There's more," she said. "I knew what a sham our relationship was, but it ended the day he came home from work and found me taking a nap. I was sick, with the flu. He ripped the covers off me and dragged me out of bed."

Absently she massaged her wrist, as if still trying to erase the memory.

"He pulled me into the living room and showed me the dust on the coffee table. How dare I be so lazy when he was working so hard to provide a living for us?"

Nick took the wrist she cradled and stroked it himself.

"I apologized to him, Nick, for being a failure. I actually apologized. Then, when I was cleaning the table with the rag he threw at me, I saw what I'd become.

"He told me it was a good thing I hadn't conceived. I was too lazy to be a good mother. When I finally gathered enough guts to call home and ask for help, I vowed I'd never get into that kind of situation again. I swore I'd never sentence myself to that kind of humiliation again."

Nick fought to keep his grip from tightening. Carefully enunciating the words, he stated, "I'm not Aaron."

"No. You're not." Her gaze dropped to his hand. "And that may be worse."

Tension returned with her honesty—the honesty he admired and yet found frustrating. "What's that supposed to mean?"

She didn't respond.

"Lilly, look at me."

Finally she did. "You're twice the man Aaron was. You made me…"

In her eyes, he saw the conflicting emotions, reluctance battling honesty, making green eyes spark and flare, reflecting the burning fire.

"You swept me away, Nick, making me forget all my resolve not to be involved with another man. And then when I…"

"Climaxed—"

Lilly nodded. "At least with Aaron, I could keep that part of me hidden. But you…" She looked at him. "You weren't satisfied until I was. I lost control, Nick. You took it.''

At least he had the same physical effect on her that she cast over him. Not that it helped any.

''Later, I told myself it was okay, that it was only a one-night stand, and I'd never have to see you again. Even when I found out I was pregnant, I thought it was okay, that you wouldn't want a family, that I was safe.''

''You were wrong.''

''Yes.'' She shook her head, dislodging the strand he'd earlier woven around his finger. ''Don't you see, Nick? It'll never work. I won't allow myself to lose control again, forget who I am, become some man's puppet.''

He put his hands on her shoulders. ''You think that's what I want? Hell, if I wanted a trophy, I'd display the ones I won in the rodeo. I don't need trophies on my mantel, and I sure as sunshine don't need one on my arm.''

''Good thing,'' she said. ''Because that's not who I am.''

''Why the hell do you think I was attracted to you in the first place? I liked your vibrancy, your openness, your willingness to live life fully. I knew what I was getting with you, Lilly. It was you I wanted, not some woman I could bully.

''And having sex isn't the same thing as losing control in a relationship,'' Nick said.

''Maybe to you, but to me, they can't be separated.''

Nick exhaled a frustrated breath. ''Aaron wasn't a real man, and he didn't know how to treat the woman he was lucky enough to have. He didn't deserve you. But let's get this straight, Lilly, once and for all. You're going to be my wife, not just someone to warm by bed and give me a hormonal release.''

Looking into the promise in the blue depths of his eyes, she very nearly did lose herself...

"I will do everything in my power to make sure you always feel you're respected as my wife. We're walking into this marriage with our eyes wide open. There are no pretensions, no love. Even after you sell your house, you can keep the money. If you don't want a joint checking account, that's fine, but I'll add you to mine and you won't have to explain your purchases. We can draw up a prenuptial agreement to protect you."

She moved away from him. "It's not that simple for me."

He dragged a hand through his hair. "You need to know something, Lilly." He crossed the room and stood looking out the window, his back to her. "Something I've never told another human being."

She paced the room, unable to contain the energy churning inside her.

"My mother brought home a man one night, when I was about five."

The rawness in Nick's voice halted her steps. She folded her arms across her chest, waiting. She'd never heard this in his tone before, a vulnerability that cut through the years and revealed pain.

"It was a couple of days before Christmas. Kurt Majors's dad took me and Kurt to the general store—they'd brought in a Santa Claus for the kids. When I crawled up on his lap, I told him that I wanted to meet my dad, find out who he was. I'd always wondered, figured Mom knew even if she'd listed his name as Unknown on my birth certificate."

Lilly ached.

"I was sure he'd like me if I could just meet him. I

promised God every night I'd be good, as long as I could have a daddy, like Kurt.''

The air in her lungs froze.

"Then my mother brought home a man. Joe Stubing was his name. I'll never forget it. He was tall, had dark hair, like mine. His eyes were blue, like mine. My mom had green eyes, so I thought…''

Lilly placed a hand over her heart. "You thought he was your father.''

Nick turned then.

His eyes were as ravaged as his voice.

"Everyone I knew had a real family. Kurt had the best. I was the only one who didn't have a father.

"I called him Daddy." Nick sneered. "I knew Santa had brought me what I wanted more than anything. I ran up to the man, hugged him around the knees. I'd never been happier in my life.''

She swallowed deeply.

"He hit me, telling me to get away from him, told me I was a no-good bastard.''

"Oh, God." Her heart wrenched. "Oh, God.''

"Gets better. Mom was appalled by my behavior. She screamed at me, slapped me herself—across the face. I never asked about my father again and I stopped believing in Santa Claus. Humiliation, Lilly? I've swallowed my share, too.''

In a moment Lilly was in his arms, her hand between them, resting on his chest. His heart raced; his jaw was tight with the effort of keeping his feelings locked away.

He lowered his head, and she offered her mouth, wanting to help him to forget. No man had ever shown her this kind of soul-baring honesty, and it stripped her defenses.

His kiss was alternately tender and reassuring, seeking and demanding.

"We'll figure out how to make it work out," he said when she teetered on the edge of surrender. "But I can't let my kid grow up without a normal family."

He didn't say another word, but left her, slamming the door behind him and making her jump.

She ached for the boy he'd been.

But the man he'd become at times terrified her.

Lilly picked up the ring and ran her finger across the golden band. She wondered why a simple piece of jewelry represented so much.

She had spent years trying to forget Aaron. Until now she thought she'd been successful. But Nick uncovered the scars that were still there, scars that sliced through time and tore a hole in the future.

Nick's words echoed inside her. She'd heard the hurt he hadn't wanted to expose and wondered how much more was there and how deeply it was buried. He'd lost his own innocence at age five, then a few years ago, lost the baby he'd thought was his, a child he loved.

He'd fight, she knew. He had no choice.

And because this was also her baby, she had to do the right thing, too.

She'd been in Shanna's nursery, had seen the book Nick had been reading. He'd even offered to stay home with the baby and take turns with feeding and diapering. If she were to ever special order a father for her child, it would be someone like Nick. He'd be a great daddy, no doubt.

Lilly held the diamond to the light. Was it possible for her to be both wife and mother without losing herself again?

Did she have any option but to try?

No matter how hard she stared into the depths of the diamond, no magical answers reflected back at her.

* * *

Nick saddled up and gave his stallion free rein.

He knew he'd exhausted every option. He couldn't force Lilly to marry him. But he'd prayed he could convince her. Honesty had been his last hope.

He'd buried the memories of his mother and that Christmas—the same year he'd gotten coal in his stocking for ruining his mother's relationship with Joe Stubing. Exposing his past had taken shovel loads of determination, but Lilly was worth it, this battle was worth it.

Her doubts were a tangible thing, something he wanted to wrap up and lock away.

That meant he had to woo her, prove he wasn't the jerk she'd once been married to.

Nick needed patience, needed to be less inflexible. They were new weapons, but hell, he wasn't proud, he'd take what he could.

Because this time, he refused to lose his child.

"Go?" she asked. "Where?"

"The flower shop."

She narrowed her eyes. He leaned against the doorjamb, not entering the room. Surely it was a good sign that she hadn't gone back to her own room and bolted the door.

Lilly put down the magazine she'd been looking at. "Why?"

"Surely you're dying to know how your sister is coping without you."

"I don't trust you, Nick."

He exhaled loudly. "No hidden motives, honest." He wondered how he didn't wince at the white lie. "Besides, I figured we'd need some more food—what with the way we both eat. Unless you'd like to stay here while I go to town...?"

"Let me get my purse."

The magazine toppled to the carpeting, falling open to the centerfold.

"One hundred and fifty ways to improve your love life?" he asked.

"I wasn't reading it," she said, avoiding his gaze while heat chased up her cheeks.

"Too bad. I was wondering what number twenty-one was."

"Number twenty-one?"

"My lucky number."

She picked up the magazine and tossed it on the coffee table. Her blush deepened and he laughed, determined to find out what number twenty-one was, and more, practice it.

Hell, maybe they could try all of the ideas, not that their love life needed a lot of improvement. That one night nearly had blown his mind. If it got any better... Nick wondered if they'd ever leave their bed.

He entered the garage, then opened the passenger door of his four-wheel-drive vehicle.

"I thought you only had the truck."

"There're a few things you don't know about me yet, Lilly. But I'll tell you anything you're interested in." He offered her a hand up.

"I can get in by myself."

"Yeah, I know. But I want to help you."

She scowled.

"Help, Lilly. Help." Dropping his voice, he added, "It's okay to accept help. Didn't your mother ever tell you your face would freeze like that?"

"Like what?"

"Scowly."

"No. I never scowled when I was growing up. And I'm not scowling now."

Their faces were only inches apart. "You're scowling."

"I'm not."

While she argued, he ran his thumb across her mouth. Her lips parted in surprise.

"Now you're not scowling. Get in the car, Lilly."

She didn't argue further.

Round one to him. He had her off balance, and he'd touched her twice without her backing up. That left him feeling pretty good.

Fifteen minutes later, the feeling was fading.

Helping her sister, Lilly was definitely in her element. There was a line of people, and while he leaned against one of the refrigerated units, she started waiting on the customers, writing up an order to send out of town, then helping Bea Hampton select just the right arrangement for her foyer.

The woman was a pain in the— With a look in the older woman's direction, he broke off the uncharitable thought. Even though Bea was picky, Lilly didn't bat an eye.

In the middle of the flower shop, women everywhere, he was suddenly self-conscious of being male and out of place. The air hung with the cloying scents of perfume and flowers.

He was excluded from conversation, until the postmistress, Bernadette Simpson, breezed in. Then he became the topic of discussion.

He decided he preferred being ignored.

"Well, young lady, has Nicholas come to his senses yet and proposed marriage?" the woman asked.

Nick looked directly at Lilly. Instinctively she'd sought his gaze and he mouthed "I'll handle it" to her.

"I'll let you in on a little secret, Bernadette," he said.

"Nothing could make me happier than to marry Lilly Baldwin. She's a beautiful woman with a heart of gold. But it's her decision. If and when there's a date set, you'll be one of the first to know."

Bernadette preened. "Promise?"

Lilly gave the woman her weekly bouquet of pink carnations, along with the book on Antony and Cleopatra, and Nick exchanged a knowing glance with his bride-to-be.

A few minutes later, the store finally emptied out. Since Beth was in the back, he and Lilly were left alone.

"Why did you do that?" she asked.

"Do what?"

"Don't play innocent with me, Nick Andrews." She came from behind the counter to poke a finger in his chest.

He'd seen her outraged, upset, hurt, tender, but this... Her eyes flashed fire and her tone held a note of tension he couldn't define.

She turned him on.

"Why did you tell Bernadette there's no date, and it's up to me if and when we get married?"

"Oh, that."

"Yeah. That. Start talking, buster."

"The date could change."

"It could?"

"I'd marry you tomorrow, if you'd agree. Who knows? We could elope."

"We're not eloping," she said.

"I could kidnap you. It worked for Kurt and Jessie. 'Course, that might make interesting copy in Miss Starr's gossip column. 'Groom holds bride hostage at church. Story on page three.'"

Lilly tipped back her head, her light brown bangs parting to fall around her forehead, framing it. After a long-suffering sigh, she looked at him. "You're impossible."

"I try."

"And what's the deal with me being a beautiful woman and nothing making you happier than us getting married?"

"You are beautiful." He caught one of her hands and lifted it to his lips.

"Nick! Stop."

"Stop what? Kissing you?"

"No, the ridiculous statements."

"Then I can kiss you?"

"Yes. No." She pulled her hand away. "You're frustrating me."

He chuckled.

"So," Beth said, coming from the back room and wiping her hands on an apron embroidered with the store's logo. "Looks like love. What're the wedding plans?"

"You, too?" Lilly asked.

"It's the bride's privilege to plan the wedding," Nick said. "And she doesn't want to set the date."

"What?" Beth demanded, eyes widened in horrified shock. "Surely you're not thinking of being a single mother?"

Nick folded his arms across his chest.

Flustered, Lilly dragged her wayward bangs back from her forehead.

"Especially when Prince Charming just told the whole town he wants to marry you."

"Thank you," he said to Beth, smiling.

"He's not Prince Charming," Lilly retorted.

"Thanks a lot."

"You be quiet." After glaring at him, she glared at her sister. "I came here to get away."

"And defy doctor's orders?"

He'd have to send Beth a gift, thanking her for the support.

Play **TIC-TAC-TOE** and get **FREE GIFTS!**

HOW TO PLAY:

1. Play the tic-tac-toe scratch-off game at the right for your FREE BOOKS and FREE GIFT!

2. Send back this card and you'll receive TWO brand-new Silhouette Desire® novels. These books have a cover price of $3.75 each in the U.S. and $4.25 each in Canada, but they are yours to keep absolutely free.

3. There's no catch. You're under no obligation to buy anything. We charge nothing — ZERO — for your first shipment. And you don't have to make any minimum number of purchases — not even one!

4. The fact is, thousands of readers enjoy receiving books by mail from the Silhouette Reader Service™ months before they're available in stores. They like the convenience of home delivery, and they love our discount prices!

5. We hope that after receiving your free books you'll want to remain a subscriber. But the choice is yours — to continue or cancel, any time at all! So why not take us up on our invitation, with no risk of any kind. You'll be glad you did!

YOURS **FREE** A FABULOUS **MYSTERY GIFT!**

We can't tell you what it is... but we're sure you'll like it!

A FREE GIFT— **just for playing**

TIC-TAC-TOE!

The Silhouette Reader Service™ — Here's how it works:

Accepting your 2 free books and gift places you under no obligation to buy anything. You may keep the books and gift and return the shipping statement marked "cancel." If you do not cancel, about a month later we'll send you 6 additional novels and bill you just $3.12 each in the U.S., or $3.49 each in Canada, plus 25¢ delivery per book and applicable taxes if any.* That's the complete price and — compared to the cover price of $3.75 in the U.S. and $4.25 in Canada — it's quite a bargain! You may cancel at any time, but if you choose to continue, every month we'll send you 6 more books, which you may either purchase at the discount price or return to us and cancel your subscription.

*Terms and prices subject to change without notice. Sales tax applicable in N.Y. Canadian residents will be charged applicable provincial taxes and GST.

If offer card is missing write to: Silhouette Reader Service, 3010 Walden Ave., P.O. Box 1867, Buffalo, NY 14240-1867

BUSINESS REPLY MAIL
FIRST-CLASS MAIL   PERMIT NO. 717   BUFFALO, NY

POSTAGE WILL BE PAID BY ADDRESSEE

SILHOUETTE READER SERVICE
3010 WALDEN AVE
PO BOX 1867
BUFFALO NY 14240-9952

NO POSTAGE
NECESSARY
IF MAILED
IN THE
UNITED STATES

"If you get married soon, you can wear a dress off the rack, instead of having to order one special."

"I'm not wearing a wedding gown. I did that once, remember?"

"Mistakes don't count," Beth said. "When do you want to go shopping?"

Lilly looked to Nick for help. Deciding to be Prince Charming, he stepped in. "She can get married in anything she wants." Personally, he preferred her in nothing at all....

"And where's your ring?" Beth asked. "I saw Jed earlier. He said you'd bought a beautiful bridal set."

"I haven't accepted it yet."

Nick saw the flush that crept up Lilly's cheeks. "When Lilly's ready, she'll show you the ring."

"Did you get one, too?"

"I intend to be an equal opportunity wedding ring wearer."

Beth smiled, then pulled her younger sister into her arms. "I'm worried about you, you know."

Nick shifted from foot to foot. He had no siblings, no parents. Except for Shane Masters and Kurt and his parents, Nick had been close to no one for most of his life. The caring family ties between Beth and Lilly didn't make him uncomfortable, just an outsider.

"He's not Aaron," Beth whispered.

Nick turned his head, pretending great interest in a flower—a daffodil, he'd been told. His nerves were stretched taut as he waited for Lilly to agree or disagree.

"I know."

"You take good care of my little sister," Beth said, looking directly into Nick's eyes. "Or you'll answer to me."

He tipped an imaginary hat. "Wouldn't think of doing anything else."

Lilly moved away when Beth said, "Go home. Doctor said you needed to rest, not work. Doesn't that fiancé of yours know any better?"

"She's tough," he commented to Lilly a couple minutes later when he was helping her back into the sports utility vehicle.

"Yes, she is," Lilly said, smiling indulgently.

For a minute, he wished he'd had a sibling who cared. "Since we're in town, shall I feed you?"

"Food?"

"As much as you can eat."

"You may live to regret those words."

"Try me," he said, sliding behind the wheel and turning the key. He slipped the manual transmission into reverse, then felt a band squeeze his chest when her hand covered his.

It may have been the first time she'd reached out to him.

"Thank you. For today…for understanding. I—I know this has to be frustrating for you."

"Lilly—"

"No, wait," she said, rushing the words together. "I need to say this. You're right about everything, about our child never having to worry who Daddy is—not that I would have let that happen. And…" she pulled back her hand and looked at him. "…I'm ready."

He eased the transmission back to neutral and set the parking brake. "Ready?"

She tied a knot in the leather strap. "To wear your ring and tell everyone we're getting married."

Life with Lilly would be many things, he knew. Dull wouldn't be one of them. Trying to contain the thrilling feeling, the possessive surge that jolted through him, he took her shoulders in his hands, touching her, he hoped, with gentleness and promise. "You won't be sorry."

She worked her lower lip between her teeth.

And then before he could stop himself, he leaned in closer, determined to take away the hurt and concern, and to hell with anyone who was looking....

Seven

Columbine Crossing Courier
"Around The Town" by Miss Starr

Miss Starr is tickled pink (or blue!) to announce that our own Lillian Baldwin is getting married to none other than rancher Nicholas Andrews!

Lilly, the co-owner of Rocky Mountain Flowers and Landscaping, will reportedly wear a long, pale pink skirt, along with a long-sleeved lace-and-satin shirt, provided by Western Occasions. Trudy Jackson will style the bride's hair for the big day. And, naturally, Lilly and Beth will be doing the flower arrangements—they should be spectacular!

Jed Burns provided the wedding bands, and I have it on good authority that Nicholas purchased a gorgeous set, complete with a one-karat, marquis-cut diamond. Miss Starr hopes to have a peek at the ring soon! As soon as she does, she promises to report her findings in this space.

The happy couple will tie the knot the second weekend of July in a private ceremony. Our very own Reverend Matthew Sheffield will be officiating the service at Nicholas's ranch house.

While he was at the post office recently, Nick was asked if he had any final words before taking the big plunge. He's quoted as saying, "I couldn't be happier."

Neither could Miss Starr! Two weddings, only months apart? Well, goodness, it just doesn't get much better than this!

Until next time, faithful readers, this is all the news you can use!

"It's bad luck to see the bride before the wedding!" Beth protested.

"I'm not a traditional sort of guy," Nick called back through the closed guest room door.

"You are when it suits you," Lilly returned.

"Come on, Lilly, have a little compassion."

"Compassion?"

She was weakening; he heard the capitulation in her tone.

"Compassion for what?"

"I'm dying of nerves out here."

He heard the two women whispering. His insides were strung tighter than a barbed-wire fence. He was desperate to reassure himself she wouldn't change her mind.

The last two weeks had been the longest of his life as he'd battled the fear that she'd walk out on him, turning her back on the things that mattered to him, the same way his mother, then Marcy. had done. It didn't matter how many times he told himself Lilly had integrity. Doubt loomed, nagging.

Over a week ago, Lilly had moved back home and gotten her house ready for sale. He'd actually dated his bride-to-be, and they'd visited every restaurant in town. Twice each.

She wore his ring, but she hadn't answered directly when he asked if she wore it even when they weren't together.

They'd settled their wedding plans—for a simple ceremony performed by Matt Sheffield. They'd be married in Nick's living room, a place where, to Nick's pleasant surprise, Lilly felt comfortable.

Kurt Majors would be his best man; Lilly's sister would be her maid of honor. Their only other guests would be Kurt's parents, Shane Masters, Jessie Majors and Lilly's parents—parents who had asked him about his intentions a hundred different ways before finally blessing the union.

"You can talk to her," Beth reluctantly conceded, cracking the door open. "But you can't see her."

Telling himself that at least she was in the guest bedroom and wasn't threatening to run away, he conceded.

Fabric rustled, then softly, very softly, Lilly said, "I'm here."

His heart skipped a beat. "I was afraid you wouldn't be." He hadn't planned to admit that to anyone, not even Kurt.

"Big, tough, macho Nick Andrews?"

He hadn't felt like any of the three in the last seventy-two hours. "I wanted to give you something before we got married."

"Nick…"

"Hold open your hand. Trust me," he added when she hesitated.

Finally she did, and he noticed her nails were painted, a subtle pink that reminded him, instantly and painfully, of the one night they'd shared. She'd had painted fingernails then, too, along with painted toenails....

His gut tightened, and he wondered how he'd survive the next few hours.

He took the old, battered penny from his pocket and placed it in her palm, then cupped her fingers closed. "It's the only thing I could think of," he said. He felt ridiculous talking to a wooden door, felt even more ridiculous now, giving the talisman to her.

"I found it when I was nine. It's been my good luck charm ever since. I wanted you to have it."

He wished he had a family heirloom to give her, something from his history that meant a lot and would stand as a symbol of their commitment to each other. But his mother had only been committed to whichever man would have her.

Lilly pulled her hand inside the room, and more than anything he wanted to see her expression. Would she laugh the way Marcy had anytime he'd attempted to express himself?

"Nick, I—I don't know what to say."

His lip curved up.

"I'm touched."

"Touched?"

The door cracked open a little wider.

"Lilly! Don't let him see you!"

She ignored her sister, pulling the door a fraction of an inch wider. Her eyes met his, and their deep depths spoke words she never would.

He breathed again. Lilly wasn't laughing at him. More, she seemed to know how much the simple gift meant.

"I'll take care of it, I promise."

He believed her.

"Thank you, Nick."

He smiled, and the stress clawing his shoulders vanished.

Unable to resist, he brought her hand to his lips and brushed a light kiss there. Even that was enough to reignite the flame that had been burning low in his gut.

"Hey, bud, minister's ready for you," Kurt said, coming down the hallway.

Kurt clamped Nick on the shoulder, and nervous energy returned, swarming through him, crawling over his skin.

"You two can kiss and talk sweet all night long, after the wedding," Kurt said. "But you've got guests. Say goodbye for now."

"Bye," she mouthed.

Before he had a chance to respond, she smiled, then shut the door.

"I gave her my lucky penny," Nick said.

Kurt whistled. "This is serious."

"She didn't laugh at me."

Kurt stared at Nick. Hard. "Did you really think she would?"

"Lilly? No."

"You're a lucky man. Beautiful woman like that, good dancer, in love with you—"

"Love?" Nick asked. "She's not in love with me."

"You gotta be kidding me."

"This wedding is because of the baby. No other reason."

Kurt muttered a word that Alice Majors would have

washed his mouth out for. "Then why'd you give her the only thing that has any meaning to you?"

"Because—ah, hell, Kurt, don't make something of it that isn't there."

"After the honeymoon, give me a buzz. We'll have a couple brewskis, talk about your stupidity."

"This isn't the real thing."

"Stubborn mule. You wouldn't know the real thing if it hit you upside the head. You hurt her and, friend or no friend, I'll take you down myself."

"You won't need to."

"Yeah. I believe you."

Kurt grinned.

Ever since Kurt had married Jessie, he'd become protective of all women. Sometimes Nick hardly recognized his old friend. Who'd have figured? Kurt, of all people. That's what love did to a man—made fools out of them.

And Nick Andrews would never be a fool again.

That resolve didn't stop his heart from giving a few extra thumps when he saw the minister and their guests in the living room.

Lilly's mother clutched a handkerchief in her hand, like she had the night she and her husband had paid Nick a little visit. His promise that he'd take care of their little girl, along with his words to Kurt, echoed in Nick's head.

He had no intention of hurting Lilly, ever. But skidding in behind that thought was the realization that he'd never believed his relationship with Marcy would end, either.

Marriage was a hell of a commitment, but one he was willing to make.

"Last chance to change your mind," Kurt said softly.

"My baby'll have my name."

Kurt grinned and jostled his friend as they headed into the living room. "Figured as much."

A few minutes later, at a signal from Reverend Sheffield, Nick turned to see Beth coming down the stairs. But he couldn't stop craning his neck for a peek at Lilly.

Standing on the landing, she didn't disappoint.

More, she stunned him.

Her eyes, wide, green and luminous, sought his. Without saying a word, she communicated how big a step this was for her.

With a nod, he tried to let her know he wouldn't let her down.

Her attempted smile fell before it fully formed.

One hand wrapped around the banister, she slowly began her descent. Her free hand clutched a small bunch—*bouquet*—of flowers, a mixture he'd insisted on choosing. He'd gotten quite an education that day, and there'd even been disagreements about what would look good together. In the end, though, he'd won.

He'd chosen heliotrope for devotion and faithfulness, stephanotis as she'd suggested for happiness in marriage, violets for faithfulness, and he'd asked for baby's breath to symbolize their commitment to their child. She'd drawn the line at traditional red roses, telling him that love didn't have anything to do with their marriage. They'd compromised on pink roses. She hadn't thought all those flowers would look good together, but he'd known they would.

He'd shocked her, though, by asking for a boutonniere, choosing a violet against an ivy leaf, signifying his promise of fidelity.

Now, looking at her, he knew he'd made the right decisions.

She wore a small hairpiece, woven with tiny rosebuds. He wanted to pluck the flowers from the rich, honeyed strands, replacing the barrette with his fingers....

He'd read in Miss Starr's column that Lilly was going

to wear a pink Western outfit, but he'd been unprepared for the way it looked on her.

It stole his breath.

Satin and lace lay against the creaminess of her skin, feminine and promising. Beneath the ankle-length skirt, he noticed the slight curve of her belly where his child grew, and his blood quickened.

Suddenly, Nick's patience vanished. Breaking ranks, he went to her, meeting her at the bottom of the stairs and offering his arm.

"Thank you," she said, looking up at him through her impossibly long lashes. "For coming to get me. It looked like a mile across the living room."

"Lilly, I'll always come to you."

Even though she held the flowers, she traced the curve of his cheek. Longing walloped him.

After today, she'd belong to him. She'd touch him more often, knowing she had that right. And he'd touch *her*....

"I like the boutonniere."

"Even if it doesn't match your dress?"

"Like you said, the meaning is more important than following tradition."

"You're admitting I'm right?"

She licked her upper lip, removing some of the pale pink gloss. He couldn't wait to kiss away the rest.

"You might have had a good idea," she conceded.

"Come on, Lilly, admit it, I was right."

"Everyone's entitled, once."

He grinned.

"The tuxedo was a good choice, too."

"I'm told I clean up well."

"You don't look too bad even when..."

"Yeah?"

"Nothing."

The pink that brushed her face matched the rosebuds in her hair.

"I'm ready," she said.

Her hand tucked in the protective nook of his arm, they walked toward the fireplace.

His heart firing an emotional response that made his words waver, Nick recited his vows—vows they'd written, along with Matt's help.

There was no promise to love or to obey. Rather, they promised they'd allow each other to be their own person. Each swore to honor and be faithful. Those were the important things, in his opinion.

Lilly repeated her oath solemnly, looking into his eyes the whole time. He slipped the ring onto her finger without her pulling away.

And then she placed a plain gold band on his finger, and the tables were turned. He felt the enormity of their commitment and recognized that this wouldn't be like his first marriage, where trust had been shattered. This would have no pretensions, and honesty would be a demand. More than anything, he'd make it work, no matter what it took.

Matt pronounced them husband and wife, then added, "You may kiss the bride."

Nick did.

And it wasn't the customary kiss she was expecting.

He took off his Stetson and enfolded her in his arms, pulling her close, closer than they'd been since the night he'd slowly stripped each piece of clothing from her body, baring her before him....

Mindless of the people around them, she responded to his kiss, rising on her tiptoes and linking her arms around his neck. Even as she surrendered, she also sought.

Kurt clapped, Beth cheered, her parents sighed, Jessie

clasped her hands over her heart, Matt Sheffield grinned indulgently and Shane shifted uncomfortably.

And when Lilly looked at Nick, it was to see a lopsided smile that could melt ice.

It didn't matter that butterflies danced a jig inside; she returned his smile. Right now, life was perfect. And she wouldn't let anything steal that feeling, not even her own doubts.

Nick lasted about half an hour before inching her into the corner and asking how long he had to put up with all these people.

"You wanted a big church wedding, remember?"

"Must have been out of my mind. So how long, Lilly?"

She licked her lips, looking over at her parents. They'd already given her their blessings. She'd mingled with their few guests.... "Now?"

With a grin, he swept her off her feet, into his arms, holding her against his chest.

"Nick! Put me down! You'll hurt your back."

"Then you'll have to massage it for me."

She grabbed hold of his lapel as he swung in the direction of the door.

"Enjoy the food and drink," he called out. "We've got a honeymoon waiting."

Amid shouts of goodwill, he carried her outside to the waiting vehicle.

Somehow it had been decorated with cans, streamers and messages, one saying Honk! Just Married!

"Payback for me doing this to Kurt's truck a few months ago," Nick muttered, trying to open the door and keep hold of her at the same time.

Even the inside of the vehicle had been decorated, with confetti and balloons.

He finally managed to get the door open, and she swept

confetti from the seat, laughing for the first time in over three months. Ever since she'd found out she was pregnant, she'd been through a hundred different emotions—rejoicing, doubt that she was good enough, wonder…. A balloon wavered with the wind and bopped her in the head. This was…fun, wonderfully uplifting.

Nick held on to her, even after he'd slid her onto the car's seat.

"What's this about a honeymoon?" she asked.

"Surprise."

"You're serious?"

"Oh, yeah."

"But I don't have any clothes."

"I've got everything you'll need."

"Everything?"

"Deodorant, toothbrush, shampoo, bikini—"

"Bikini?"

"You'll need it." He quirked a brow. "Unless you don't mind skinny-dipping?"

"As in naked?"

"Suits me fine."

"When I'm already starting to show?"

"Lady, I can't think of anything sexier."

She shivered with an illicit thrill. If she wasn't careful, this man might steal her heart. "Where are we going?" she asked, the words almost a squeak.

"The hot springs."

"I haven't been there since I was a kid."

"Then you're in for a treat." He closed the door, then battled the balloons himself as he climbed in beside her.

"Nick?"

"Hmm?"

"You didn't mention that you packed me any clothes or pajamas."

"Man, I knew I forgot something."

"Are you serious?"

"No. But I like the way you blush."

Gathering the balloons, she tied the strings to the gearshift, then tried to keep the colorful array away from the rearview mirror.

They made it less than a mile before Nick saw the flashing lights behind him and pulled over.

He rolled down his window, only to have a very determined balloon elude Lilly's attempts to catch it. It flew out and snagged on Sheriff Spencer McCall's badge. A loud explosion cracked the air, then the red remains fell to the ground.

"Sorry 'bout that," Nick said.

Lilly laughed. Nick turned to her, fighting his own grin, warming her heart. It was a moment she'd never shared with another man. Like it or not, she was forming memories with him, of him. And they slowly replaced the ones Aaron had left behind. Aaron wouldn't have found any of this amusing and would have been furious at being pulled over.

More and more, she saw how different the men were.

"Don't tell me, you won't be coming to the boys' poker night anymore," Spencer said, pulling out his citation book.

"Not unless Lilly gets tired of me being home."

"Sorry, Spence. You'll have to find someone else."

"First Kurt, now you." Spencer shook his head. "What's this town coming to? As long as we've still got Shane, there's still hope."

"I think you're pretty safe there," Nick said.

"Just wanted to congratulate you both. Oh, and keep those balloons out of the way of the mirrors. Wouldn't want you driving while distracted."

"Yes, sir, Sheriff McCall."

Spencer tipped his hat, pocketed his citation book, then headed back to his cruiser.

"What next?" Lilly asked, swallowing a laugh.

She found out soon enough.

The hot springs resort was celebrating Christmas in July. Inside, Tom and Gwen Morgan had decorated the lobby and restaurants with trees and lights, and there was a colorful array of brightly wrapped packages beneath the trees.

Carols drifted softly from hidden speakers, and the fragrant scents of pine and potpourri wafted through the air. Candles burned and flickered in brass and silver sconces, making their honeymoon truly feel like a celebration.

"This is fabulous," Lilly said to Nick.

"Hope it's as good as going out of town for a few days."

"Even better," she said, the magic of the season drifting over her, even though the actual holiday was several months away.

"We'll have to spoil the kid on Christmas morning," he said.

"Wouldn't dream of doing it differently."

She laughed when he swept her into his arms, her skirt sneaking up past her ankles and hanging over his tux. Gwen herself hurried in front of them to open the door, and, wishing them well, disappeared so he could carry his bride over the threshold in private.

He paused there, giving Lilly a kiss and a look that made her feel so very special. With a skip in her pulse, she closed the door behind them.

A pile of pink feathers graced the middle of the bed in the honeymoon suite. "Feathers?"

"Number twenty-one," he said.

Her mouth dried. "Number twenty-one?"

"From the magazine article. Thought we'd give it a try."

She remembered number twenty-one. It involved a feather, the feet, and the man moving the feather upward in slow, circular motions....

"Number seventy-three was pretty good, too," he said. She dragged her gaze away from the feathers.

"You do it in waist-deep water."

"Waist deep?"

"You like water, don't you?"

"Yes, but—"

"We've got our own private springs, right off the room. And you won't need a bathing suit for number seventy-three." He opened the drapes, showing her a courtyard, fenced in by an adobe wall.

Steam shivered from the water, billowing skyward, and potted flowers bloomed along the walls. In honor of Christmas in July, the two large evergreens were decorated with white lights that glowed even in the sunshine.

"Nick, it's beautiful."

"You pleased?"

"Oh, yes." Lost in the view and by the sight of Eagle's Peak rising to flirt with high cirrus clouds in the distance, she also admitted, "Nervous, too."

He placed his hands reassuringly on her shoulders, and turned her toward him. "We'll do things at your pace. If you don't want to make love tonight, we won't."

"And tomorrow night?"

"Lilly, we'll make love when you want to."

"But—"

"Listen to me," he interrupted. "I want to make love to my wife, want you to know you're my wife in every meaning of the word."

His gaze dropped. Leisurely he perused her whole body,

from her eyes to her toes. Even without a touch, she felt that warmth in her stomach again, a feeling her ex-husband had never been able to arouse.

"But I won't do anything you don't want. I know you don't want to lose control, but I'll still prove that you can give yourself to me without losing yourself like you did with Aaron. And I'll tell you this, Lilly...I won't make love to you until you ask me to."

A hot chill chased up her spine, then down again. "And if I don't?"

"You're responsive and giving. You'll ask, Lilly. You'll ask."

Her toes curled, knowing he was right.

"You touched me earlier, on the cheek. Like this." He snagged one of her wrists and moved her hand to his face.

She stroked her fingers down the strong line of his jaw, feeling the subtle, untamed shadow already growing there.

"Now feel this."

She gasped, but he only moved her hand beneath his tuxedo jacket to his chest, pressing her palm against the rhythm of his heart.

"Just your touch does that to me."

"You're joking."

"No, ma'am, I'm not. And your voice..."

"My voice? I was told I sound like a nagging old woman."

He actually laughed. "More like an angel offering a slice of heaven."

"Now you're teasing."

"You think so?" He only pressed her hand closer. "Then why am I still responding to you?"

She was saved from answering by a knock on the door.

"Room service!"

"Be right back."

He handed some money to the waiter, then returned to her with a magnum of champagne in a silver bucket and two crystal glasses.

"I can't drink," she apologized.

"It's nonalcoholic."

"Do you think of everything?"

"I'm trying."

She was falling. No doubt about it. When he wanted to, Nick could charm. He had that first night, until she'd lost all common sense.

She couldn't allow that to happen again.

With a flash of insight, she knew she couldn't stop it....

After he shucked his jacket from his shoulders and draped it across the back of a chair, he loosened his string tie, allowing the ends to dangle against the white of his shirt. Nick removed the studs from the cuffs, then rolled up the sleeves, exposing his forearms and the dark hair growing there.

And she couldn't look away....

He uncorked the bottle and poured two glasses and offered one to her. He tipped his flute in her direction. "To us—the three of us."

She clinked the rim of her glass against his, then took a sip. To Lilly, it didn't matter that the champagne wasn't alcoholic; she was nervous and giddy, tingly inside.

At Kurt and Jessie's wedding reception, she'd blamed the two drinks she'd had for her reaction to Nick. Now she knew differently.

Nick moved to the bed and sat on it, sweeping the feathers to one side. "Come here."

Her knees locked.

He waited, saying nothing.

Long moments dragged.

Finally he looked at her earnestly, eyes open and honest.

"I've already told you you'll have to beg me to make love to you."

"Beg?"

"Beg," he confirmed, in that gruff, manly tone that sent shivers through her.

"That won't happen."

"Wanna bet?"

Nick in this mood might be her undoing, she realized. Charming and teasing? She didn't stand a chance.

"Come here," he repeated.

Her resolve splintered.

"Bring your drink," he said, when she went to slip it onto the dresser.

She sat near him, her legs tucked beneath her in proper, ladylike fashion. But she couldn't forget the feathers. They loomed in her peripheral vision, a constant reminder of what he wanted to do....

"You're a beautiful bride."

Looking at him, she laughed. "There you go again with the ridiculous statements."

"I don't make ridiculous statements."

She forgot to breathe.

A frown burrowed between his dark eyebrows.

He was serious. Heaven help her, she'd never had a man think she was beautiful before.

He rubbed the pad of his thumb down her nose. "Perfect."

She tried to laugh but couldn't get enough air.

"And your lips..." He continued his exploration. "Perfectly shaped."

"Thanks to lipstick and liner."

"I've kissed off the lipstick and liner before, Lilly. Can't fool me. I've seen every one of your secrets—exposed them all."

"So you know my flaws, as well."

"Yeah, like the fact you haven't begged me to make love to you yet."

Tension scattered to the corners of the room. "Told you, it isn't going to happen."

"So you did. And your throat…"

"It's an ordinary throat," she protested, clutching the crystal stem of her glass even tighter.

"That's where you're wrong."

"I'll bite," she said.

"I wish."

Tension drowned her again.

"Remember how I held your hand on my heart?"

She nodded, unable to forget.

With his fingers, he stroked the sides of her throat. Her head eased to the side, even against her will.

Nick paused, his forefinger resting on the throb of her pulse. "I can tell," he said softly, leaning forward to scoop her hair into his free hand, "if you're affected by me."

She brought her head forward and met his eyes.

"I can tell if you like this…." He glanced a kiss across her jawbone.

"And this."

He dusted his knuckles across her lips.

Her mouth opened.

She was losing.

His touch on the throbbing pulse in her neck warmed her skin, and her eyes drifted shut.

"Or maybe this." He lowered his head and kissed the hollow of her throat.

She jerked and the champagne swished.

Then, with a whisper, he swept his hand across the front of her dress. Her eyes opened to see that his were hooded. This wasn't a game to him. He was serious and intent, and her control was slipping as she slid into dangerous territory.

"It's a nice throat," he said. "Very nice. And these rosebuds in your hair. They're pretty. Can I take them out?"

Her mind swam.

"Can I?"

"Yes."

He needed no second invitation.

Bobby pins tinkled onto the bedspread, followed by the hairpiece Beth had made.

"Much better," he said, approvingly, his fingers in her hair as he combed out the layers, leaving the strands curling around her face, her neck. "Looks wild."

"I'm not wild."

"Yeah, you are."

"Plain, staid—"

"Anything but," he corrected.

He was so close, not even an inch away. His scent engulfed her, that of mountain nights and passion, a combination that played havoc with her feminine senses.

He drew her hair forward, framing her face. "Beautiful," he said, "no doubt."

For that moment, for the first time in her life, she believed it, believed him.... That she had an effect on Nick, a man most single women in town were interested in, staggered her.

Right now, he wasn't making her feel as though this was a marriage he hadn't wanted, that she was only an obligation.

To stop the insanity rampaging through her, she reminded herself that if there were no baby, she would have never seen him again. This was a marriage for his convenience. Nothing more.

And yet a wayward part of her insisted he was looking at her as if he wanted her, not some other, nameless woman. *Her.*

But wasn't the availability of sex one of the main reasons men got married? Nick made it clear he was no different in that respect.

Still, he'd also said that if they made love it would be under her terms and she'd name them.

A hundred, maybe a thousand, conflicting thoughts dashed through her mind.

"I like this outfit," he said.

"I didn't want to wear a white dress."

"You made the perfect choice. I remember..."

She said nothing.

"At Kurt and Jessie's wedding, you wore a black dress, a hot little number with an open back."

"I'd just bought it. I'd never worn anything like that before."

"It was perfect. And underneath it, you had on black panties and not much else."

"Nick!"

"And that makes me wonder..."

"What I have on underneath this."

"Yes."

Who was this daring woman? she wondered. She'd never teased a man, never engaged in any sexual banter.

"Yeah. So, you going to tell me, or do you want me to guess?"

Her nerve was running out.

"I'll guess," he said a minute later. "Give me your glass."

"My glass?"

"I don't want you spilling."

Nick, keeping her off balance as always, moved away,

then grabbed pillows and piled them against the wooden headboard.

"What does this have to do with you guessing?"

"Wait and see. Okay, now move up here." He offered his hand.

A few seconds later, she lay back comfortably among the pillows.

"Shoes," he said.

"What about them?"

"They've got to go."

She sucked in a breath as he tugged off the first shoe. His lucky penny fell out, and he slid it onto the bedstand. "I wanted to keep it with me," she explained. "For luck."

He smiled, and she was glad she had kept it.

Nick took her other shoe and tossed it on the floor alongside the first.

"What...?" she asked.

He didn't answer, but shifted until he was at the end of the bed, her feet in his lap.

"You're peeking!" she protested.

"That wouldn't be fair." He started rubbing her feet with long strokes.

"You have all night to stop doing that," she said.

"It'd be easier if you took off your nylons."

"I'm not going to start undressing for you."

"It was worth a try. White."

"White?"

"Underwear. Cotton. Briefs that cover you all the way to your navel."

She laughed.

"Black."

"Underneath pale pink?"

"Good point. Bright red."

She shook her head. "It'd show through."

"Beige."

She rose up on her elbows to look at him. "Beige?"

"Since you matched at Kurt and Jessie's wedding, you probably did the same thing for our wedding. You've gotta be wearing pink, Lilly."

Her shoulders fell back into the pillows.

"So tell me about the panties. They cotton? Heard cotton's the most breathable fabric."

She hadn't intended to relax. Didn't want to. But she was. "You heard that, did you?"

"Read it in your magazine."

"Just what else did you read?" she asked.

"I saw that in next month's issue they'll have an article on a hundred and fifty ways a man can drive a woman wild in bed."

She'd bet a foot rub was number one.

"Thought you should subscribe to the magazine."

"Nick, you don't need any tips."

He stopped, midstroke. "No?"

She hadn't meant to say that.

"What did you like best that night?"

Her toes tingled.

"I'll do it again, if I just know how you like to be pleasured."

She was drowning in a sea of her own sensuality.

"Satin," he said.

She frowned, trying to follow him.

"Your panties. Are they satin?"

"Yes."

His growled response was low and deep and sexy.

She shivered.

"Tell me about your bra—does it cover your breasts?"

"It's a demi-cup."

"Meaning?"

"It barely covers…" She wished she had her wineglass, anything to hold on to.

"Your nipples?"

Instantly her nipples hardened and her breasts felt full, pushing against the fabric of her bra. "Right."

He started rubbing her feet again, but she felt the tension bunched in his thighs, heard it gathered in his words. "So, is it lacy?"

"Yes."

"Maybe this wasn't a good idea," he said, his tone scratchy, like something dragged over an icefall. "Told you there was nothing dull and staid about you, Lilly. Underneath the exterior you show the world is a woman wanting to experience life—all of it. You proved that at Kurt and Jessie's wedding."

He saw too much. Maybe that was one of the reasons he frightened her so much.

Nick kept up those incredible motions, then circled a little higher, to her ankles, then her calves.

The skin of his work-roughened fingertips snagged on her silky hose. "Sorry," he said.

"You were right. I should have taken them off."

"You still can."

"Nick—"

"I'd like to help you relax, rub your shoulders, your back. But there's no pressure, Lilly. Your pace."

He was asking so much more, she knew. If she started to undress for him, she wondered if she'd stop…. "Were you serious when you said I'd have to beg?"

He looked at her intently, as if trying to read on her face the answer she wanted to hear. "No, I'd never make you beg."

"Then…?"

His hand closed around her leg. "You'll have to let me

know, Lilly. It may be one of the most difficult things I've ever done, but I swear, unless you ask, unless you say yes, unless you nod, I won't make love to you.''

Having that kind of power was equally terrifying and thrilling. She had to take responsibility for her own actions, couldn't claim she'd been swept away, that she wasn't thinking. She'd done that once before; obviously he didn't want her running again. ''If I take off my panty hose, will you promise not to watch?''

''Lilly, you tempt me.'' The words rumbled and a pulse ticked along his jawline. ''I'll turn my head.''

She slid from the bed, wriggled out of the constricting nylons and dropped them on the floor, next to her shoes.

''Are you wearing a slip?''

''Yes.''

''Then you can take off your skirt, too.''

When she sighed, he added, ''Look, I'll be fully dressed. How dangerous can that be?''

Horribly, she knew.

Yet the idea of a massage tantalized her. She'd had a full body massage once, and nearly melted. And this man was her husband. If he was offering a massage, she wouldn't be foolish enough to turn it down. Bravely, before she could change her mind, she took off her skirt, then unbuttoned the long-sleeved shirt, a confection of lace, satin and femininity. She left on her slip and camisole, however, as if they would be any protection....

She rejoined him on the bed, her pulse rushing at the sound of him sharply drawing a breath.

''Lovely,'' he murmured, approvingly.

She drew a pillow against her chest.

''Turn over,'' he said.

She did, feeling the glide of his hands, the way he gently worked at the muscles. After a couple of minutes, she forgot to be nervous. It would be easy to imagine he didn't threaten her.

That thought vanished when he skimmed her inner thighs and then worked on her buttocks.

Warmth—nothing to do with relaxation—gushed through her, tightening her insides.

"Relax," he whispered, as if reading her mind.

It was too late. She'd felt his touch, remembered her reaction to his touch, wanted his touch.

She froze, her nipples tight buds, her breasts heavy, her stomach knotted with anticipation and—heaven help her— demand. She wanted him, every bit as much as she wanted not to want him.

"Lilly?"

Her first time with Nick had been a one-night stand, her response unusual. So why then did she feel this urge to hold him, to ask him to make love to her?

"Do you want me to stop?"

"No. Yes."

"Turn over, look at me."

Reluctantly she did.

"Talk to me."

"I'm…" *Dying of embarrassment.* This was a culmination of so many things—of his gentleness, his intensity, his patience, his touch.… It was about so much more than sex.

"Lilly?"

"I can't ask," she murmured.

Silence, unbroken except for their rapid breathing, filled the room.

"What are you saying? That you want me to stop touching you?"

"No."

"Lilly, I didn't do this as a way to get you hot so that I could have sex with you."

"I know. I just didn't know that I could really…that is…" She tried to drop her chin, only to have him tighten his grip. "I actually want to make love."

His eyes narrowed. "Lilly, I'm flesh and blood. And what you're saying to me is making me hard, fast. If you want to make love, say so."

Telling herself this was only to make their temporary marriage work, she licked her parched lips.

"Is that a yes?" he asked, his hand shaking where he held her.

He wasn't giving her any place to run or hide. And she knew how much her answer mattered to both of them.…

Gazing deeply into his eyes, she said honestly, "Yes."

The look he gave her, coupled with the slow, steamy smile, made her gulp.

"This is what you do to me."

This time he didn't place her palm on his chest, but below his waist, where she felt him pushing against her hand.

He desired her. With that realization came a rush of power. She'd never experienced anything like this, never imagined having the tables turned so far that this didn't feel like a weekly responsibility.

He released her chin. Then, standing, he pulled her to her feet, slowly moving his hand down to brush the tip of her breast through the fabric of the camisole.

She exhaled the small amount of breath remaining in her lungs and then reached for his tie, tugging on the ends and letting it swish to the floor, on top of her clothes.

"It'll be my pleasure," he said, snagging the hem of the silky garment and lifting it over her head.…

Eight

Lilly gasped when he dropped her camisole onto the carpeting in a splash of silk. He nearly did the same at the sight of her. His insides were wound tight with demand. But he'd wait. Even if it was the hardest damned thing he'd ever done.

She started to bring up her hands to cover herself, but he caught them.

"Don't," he said.

With great reluctance, her eyes met his, seeking reassurance.

"I want to see you, all of you."

"But—"

"It's nothing we haven't done before."

"Not like this," she said.

"I don't want you diving under the covers or turning out the lights."

"It's daylight," she said. She gave him a smile, but it wavered.

"The thought's still the same," he countered. "Is that what you really want?" He held both her wrists with one hand and tipped back her chin with his thumb. "To hide like you did before?"

She closed her eyes.

"Don't shut me out, Lilly."

"No..." she admitted, the word drawn out. "That's not what I want."

"Then let me see you, touch you, taste you...."

After a shiver that chased goose bumps up her arms, she obviously forced herself to relax.

Nick released her hands and she dropped them to her sides. "Lace," he said approvingly. The demi-cup supported her, revealing the creaminess of her breasts. Through the pale pink fabric, he saw the rise of her nipples. She was aroused, like him....

He swallowed.

Gently he drew the abrasive lace across one tip, hearing her cry out. She *was* sensitive, more so than the last time they'd been together. "Will you unfasten your bra for me?"

Slowly, without saying a word, she reached for the clasp.

Nick watched, feasting on the sight of her.

She dropped the undergarment.

He admired her when she raised her chin, shaking her hair back from her face and meeting his gaze.

He couldn't hold her eyes longer than a second; he had to see her body. "Your breasts are fuller."

She drew her lips between her teeth.

"Lovely," he said. "And the area around your nipples, it's darker."

"Yes."

Cupping her breasts with his palms, he brushed his thumbs across the tips. Her head swayed to one side, light brown hair cascading across her neck.

He replaced his thumbs with the sweep of his mouth, and she moaned quietly. Then he drew one peak into his mouth, suckling there.

Lilly grabbed him, her fingers digging into his shoulder blades and grasping his dress shirt.

It was no longer enough. "I want you naked for me," he said, his voice scratchy.

His fingers feeling more like thumbs, he fumbled with undressing her the rest of the way, sliding her slip and underpants past her hips and down her thighs.

She kicked free of the fabric and reached for him again.

"Wait," he said. "Let me look."

She did.

He started with her feet and slowly worked his way up, looking at the curve of her hips, then the slight swell of her stomach. He looked at her breasts, the way the areolas had darkened and the nipples had lengthened.

Then looking wasn't enough and he touched, placing his hand on her abdomen and feeling....

When her knees buckled, he slid an arm beneath her legs and carried her to the bed.

Tonight of all nights, he wanted to be the experienced seducer. He'd had patience that first night. Maybe that was because she'd hidden beneath the covers and he hadn't seen her proudly standing before him, hadn't noticed her reactions, which said she was ready for him.

Instead, she'd kept the light off and he'd used all his skills to pleasure her, thinking of her and only her.

Now...

Now she'd lived beneath his roof, kept a door closed between them at night, even though he'd heard her shower, known when she was washing, rubbing a towel across her damp body, changing her clothes....

He'd had weeks of feeling desire—and had been celibate. That particular brand of patience wouldn't last much longer, he knew. *He* wouldn't last much longer.

"This isn't fair," she protested. "You're still fully dressed."

"I'll take care of that right away."

She wiggled, pulling the bedspread down and pushing aside the sheets, even as she watched him.

He needed to be inside her.

And the demand was urgent.

Seconds later, she scooted over, and he joined her on the bed.

Daylight streamed through the closed curtains. There'd be no secrets between them, just the way he wanted it. This wasn't a one-night stand. It had to be right. "You're perfect," he said. "Just enjoy...."

Propped on one elbow, he stroked the inside of her calf, going a little higher with each caress, nearing her knee. She kept her thighs together, and the sound of her breathing filled his ears. Not soft, but ragged; not relaxed, but tense.

"Your pace," he reminded her. "I won't do anything until you're ready."

Slowly she parted her legs. He continued those motions; then, when he neared the juncture of her thighs, she tensed again, digging her heels into the mattress and tightening her buttocks.

Her pace might kill him.

Nick waged an internal debate. He moistened his thumb. Then slowly, deliberately, he swept it across her most sensitive spot.

"Nick!"

Even though he'd promised, he repeated the act.

She shivered.

"Tell me, Lilly. Tell me to stop, or tell me to continue."

Her hands formed fists at her sides. "Let's just get it over with."

"Nope," he said. "Doesn't work that way. Not with me. I want you wet and willing."

She gulped. "But—"

"That's the deal. You're not sacrificing yourself for me." He moved subtly, keeping a light pressure *there*.... "I'm not your ex-husband." He refused to say the man's name. "And this isn't a weekly obligation for me to get rid of my excess testosterone."

"Ah..."

"This is about pleasure. Mine, but yours, too. I want you to let me know how you want it, and I won't let you run or hide from me, from yourself. Do you like this?" A few seconds later, he stopped.

She dug her heels deeper into the mattress, but it wasn't because she was getting tense, it was because she was seeking his touch. Greedily, he wanted her even hungrier.

"Tell me what you want." He looked at her, saw that her nipples were still hard and that her lower lip was swollen from her worrying it.

"I liked that."

"What?"

"Nick!"

"Tell me, Lilly."

"You know... That."

He didn't move.

"The way you were touching me."

"Like this?" He slipped his thumb between her folds, and this time she was moist.

"Yes!"

"Faster? Slower? More gently? More pressure? How?" When she didn't answer, he stopped again.

For the first time since he'd known her, she muttered a mild curse. He grinned. She was losing that cherished control, and he liked it.

"Harder," she whispered.

A little at a time, he increased the pressure against her, rubbing, feeling, his finger slipping on her moisture.

When she started to wiggle beneath him, her breaths coming in shortened bursts, he moved away, cradling his palm around one of her breasts and closing his mouth around its distended tip.

She lifted her hips, calling out his name.

He could have taken her over the edge, he knew, but he wanted her there awhile longer. When she came, he wanted it to be totally, completely.

He wanted her to know she was his.

That thought rocked him. Unwelcome and intense, it twisted in his heart. She carried his baby, and that was that. At least that was all he wanted it to be....

Turning to her other breast, he laved it with the same kind of attention. Gently he ran his teeth across the top.

"Now!" she said, grabbing him. "Now, Nick. Make love to me. I want you inside me."

Physical demand clawed at him. Her urgency driving him, he moved between her legs and entered her—deeply—with a single, smooth stroke.

She was wet, like he'd wanted. She was welcoming, like he'd hoped.

With her hands on his back, fingers pressed against his spine, he began to move, feeling her tighten around him, drawing the response he was trying desperately to hold back.

His strokes intensified, and her breathing grew labored.

Focusing on her—his wife—he kissed her forehead and whispered an endearment, something he'd never, ever done before. He drove deep and she lifted her hips, whimpering like she'd done their first night together.

Gratitude for what she'd given him crashed through him, and so did his climax.

Seconds later, he was spent, physically.

But it went beyond that, he knew. It was an emotional release, too.

Their lovemaking had been crucial in setting the stage for their entire married life.

Slowly his breathing returned to normal. He'd worked up a sweat, and it clung to him, like the sweetness of her scent.

He moved them around so that she lay snuggled on his outstretched arm, against his body.

Softly she said, "You were serious. You didn't enter me until I begged you to."

"I wanted you to want it as much as I."

"I did."

Her tousled hair covered her eyes but he didn't move it, determined not to stop what she was saying. "Surprised?"

"At Kurt and Jessie's wedding, I wanted you but I've never been so—I don't know—aroused, that I'd ask a man to make love to me."

He moved her hair aside then and looked into her eyes. "You're my wife, Lilly. Anything you want is yours."

She shivered.

"But what I want is to discover you."

She laughed. "You just did."

"Nah, I just figured out one way to make you come. I want to know a dozen more."

"A dozen?" Her mouth formed a circle in shock.

He slipped a finger inside, pressing the pad against her tongue. "At least."

Her eyes wide, she closed her lips. Then she suckled.

And he figured she'd just found the first way to make *him* shatter.

"You're hungry?"

Pulling a pillow against her chest, she nodded.

"Again?"

"Yes."

"So am I," he said, reaching for her.

She laughed. "For food, Nick, real food."

"Okay, okay," he grumbled. "I'll feed you so you can keep up your stamina."

"Me? Why would I need to do that?"

"Because…" He wound his fingers in her hair and drew the strands toward him, inhaling the scent of the herbal shampoo she used, as well as the lingering hints of rose. "I'm not finished with you yet."

"But we've already… Twice."

"Third time's a charm."

His voice had lazy and husky undertones, something she'd never heard from him before. They sent a renewed awareness down her insides.

Nick hadn't been lying when he said this was far more than a quick release of hormones, more than her fulfilling her duty so that he could be more comfortable. Her responses seemed to matter to him. Her pleasure mattered.

He had been demanding of her, more than she'd believed possible. She'd never told a man what she wanted, how she wanted it and what felt good. But Nick asked all those questions, and more, refused to take silence as an answer.

Yet for everything he demanded, he gave equally in return.

"Okay, food," he said, as if reminding himself. He released her and reached for the telephone on the nightstand. "One of everything on the room service menu?"

"What? You're not eating?"

"Gotcha. Two of everything on the menu."

While he placed the order, she made a dash to the bathroom, searching for a robe. His low whistle of approval followed her.

Pulling the thick white terry garment from a hook behind the door, she cinched the belt, then caught sight of herself in the mirror.

Her hair framed her face in wild disarray, the layers tousled. Her cheeks were rosy, and a small burn from his afternoon shadow lingered on the side of her neck. Her lips were swollen and reddened and sparks of hazel lit her green eyes. She looked *different*, well loved.

Aaron had never had this effect on her.

She shivered.

As threatening as Aaron had been, he didn't begin to compare with Nick. Aaron never wanted anything from her, Nick did—her participation, enjoyment, her total capitulation. If the relationship with Aaron had worried her, *this* terrified her.

"Doing okay?"

Nick came up behind her, gloriously naked and comfortable with his body. He nuzzled her neck.

She saw them both in the mirror, her body dwarfed by his rugged six-foot-one frame. His shoulders were twice as broad as hers, and when he wrapped his arms around her, she felt both his protection and the potential for his fury.

She wasn't able to forget he was a man who'd thrown his first wife out in the street, a man who'd settle for nothing less than total honesty, a man who would never love her.

"Hmm?" he asked, kissing her throbbing pulse.

"It's just..." How did she say what she didn't dare?

"Yeah?"

She closed her eyes, shutting out his potent image and hoping that she'd also be able to banish his assault on her senses.

"I'm listening."

"I keep wondering what I got myself into."

He placed another kiss, followed by yet one more, then another....

Having her eyes closed only made it worse. Without her sight, the sense of touch flared powerfully.

She reached up, holding him around the forearm. She was aware of his texture—of muscle and sinew—and filled with the knowledge that there was no escape.

He was so much more man than she knew how to handle.

"You're not sorry we made love?"

"No."

"Open your eyes, Lilly, I want to see your reflection."

Slowly she did.

He was looking at her seriously, completely focused on her.

"What's bothering you?"

"Are you a mind reader?"

"Don't need to be when you're frowning."

She smiled a little.

"Talk to me," he urged.

"I'm wondering what we'll do when we have arguments."

His arms tightened around her, but it felt reassuring. "We'll talk them through."

"And what if I don't live up to your expectations?"

Slowly he released her and turned her to face him. Cupping her face in his hand, he said, "You'll never disappoint me, Lilly, as long as you're honest, as long as you put our child first."

"I will always do that."

"I know. I know."

He kissed her then, a deep, passionate kiss that dispelled her doubts.

A knock on the door forced them apart.

He grabbed the matching robe, then disappeared.

The scent of musky male hung in the air, seeming to wrap around her just as his arms had done.

She'd thought she was prepared for this marriage, for their honeymoon. After all, she'd made love to him before.

But then she'd had nothing at stake emotionally. She'd hidden beneath blankets and sheets, been daring in the dark, then vanished at dawn.

Now he held her future in his work-roughened palms. His promises were little comfort.

She heard the murmur of voices, then the door to their suite closed.

Lilly splashed water on her face, then went into the parlor. The small table nearly groaned under the weight of the food he'd ordered.

"Nick! I was joking."

"Figured I'd save the waiter a trip in another hour."

If he hadn't ordered everything, he'd come close, from fresh fruit to cheese and crackers, sandwiches and a decadent chocolate dessert.

Not needing a second invitation, she tucked her feet beneath her on the chair and allowed him to fill a plate for her.

She'd been right to break it off with him, she realized. He could charm when he wanted to, as he had at Kurt and Jessie's wedding. She'd have lost herself before she could count to three—quite happily. And when she learned what kind of man he really was and that he'd always try to control her, she would have been devastated—if she'd have given her heart to him.

It was better it ended this way, with him saying he'd never love her, no pretenses.

"It's called Death by Chocolate," he said, sinking his fork into the triple layer cake.

"I think I'd die with a smile on my face," she said.

"Open your mouth."

Trustingly, she did, closing her lips around the fork. Rich, dark chocolate smoothed across her tongue, and she gave a tiny moan of delight.

"I've heard that sound before."

Allowing her taste buds to savor, she looked up at him through her lashes.

"In bed," he said. "Which is where I'm going to take you soon. Death by chocolate is right."

She finally swallowed, but when she reached for a second bite, he stole the fork. "Not until I've enjoyed, too."

He kissed her, long and deep, sweetness blending with his power and taking her breath.

Ending the kiss slowly, he stood. Hands on her shoulders, he drew her up, then said, "Undress me."

Her eyes widened.

"I want you to touch me," Nick said, "feel me, know what you do to me."

Her heart turned over. "I don't know what to do."

"I'm only wearing one thing."

So was she, and now, with him watching her, she was consciously aware of that and the way the nubby material suddenly seemed to abrade her.

Unsure, blood racing, she gingerly took hold of the belt at his waist and worked the knot free. The ends fell from her nerveless fingers, then she parted his robe, reaching to shuck it from his shoulders.

He was ready for her.

Her toes sank into the carpeting.

Hard and angular everywhere, he was all male. And he was her husband.

Hardly able to talk, she asked, "Now what?"

"Feel me, explore my body. Know me as intimately as I already know you."

Nervousness, as well as adrenaline, rushed through her.

Rigid, he stood there, looking at her. Waiting.

Wetting her lips, she whispered, "Turn around."

After raising a speculative brow, he slowly complied.

He'd seen her; now she drank her fill of him. Ravenous, she wanted more than the quick, embarrassed peep she'd sneaked when he'd moved around the suite.

Silence draped the room, and tension quickened her breathing.

Shaking, she reached out, running the tips of her fingers across his shoulder blades. She explored the contours, the feel of his flesh. Skimming the length of his spine, she stopped at the small indentation right above his buttocks.

Chickening out, she ran her hands up his back, then rubbed his shoulders before feathering her fingers through the thick strands of his dark hair.

His head fell forward as she outlined, from the back, the shell of his ear.

Amazingly, warmth spread through *her*.

"Turn around again," she said, the words a little squeak.

He did, with a grin that sent shock waves into her mid-section.

Instead of taking over, he patiently waited.

Face-to-face, this was more difficult. She didn't let that stop her.

Her thumbs laced together, she moved her palms down his chest, exploring the small rise of his nipples buried in the downy mat of chest hair. He jerked. Feeling the headiness of her own power, she repeated the motion. ''Do you like that?''

He answered with a guttural groan.

Testing him, she gently scraped a nail across one nipple, then the other. His reaction was instantaneous and he thrust out toward her.

Enthralled, she reached for him, closing her hand. Watching the shallow rise and fall of his chest, she stroked him.

He grabbed her upper arms. ''Enough.''

She didn't think so. Despite the hot blue ice in his eyes, she tightened her grip.

''Lilly, I'm warning you....''

She didn't heed it.

She felt the change in him, as he became fuller, like her breasts did when he held them. ''You told me before that you liked this.''

''I do.'' His head fell back.

''So enjoy.''

Nick clamped his hand around her wrist. ''This will be over in thirty seconds, if you don't stop.''

Galvanized by the raw note in his voice, the primal beat beneath her palm, she said, ''That's okay.''

''No...it's...not.'' He increased the pressure on her until she let go, then he drew a shaky breath before turning the tables, carrying her to the bed and dropping her in the middle of it. ''Liked that, did you?'' he asked.

She smiled shyly.

''Then we'll make love a different way.''

He lay beside her, then took hold of her waist and drew her on top of him.

"Ah, Nick..."

"Put your knees on either side of me."

Swallowing her reluctance, she nodded, her hair falling around her face.

He touched her most sensitive spot and she arched, stifling a sharp gasp. *She wanted him.* Finding courage, she followed his lead, curving her hand around his shaft, then slowly lowering herself onto him.

He filled her, stretched her, made her ache and burn.

Then he reached for her breast and teased the tip. She wiggled, trying to avoid the arcing sensations, but only made it worse.

She closed her eyes, seeing shooting sparks in the darkness. He lifted his hips and she rode the motion, welcoming him deeper.

Together they found a rhythm as a whirling kaleidoscope wound through her body.

She'd never experienced anything like this—so full, and hovering just this side of the edge.

Reaching up, he cupped her breasts, then, on her downward motion, squeezed her nipples.

"Nick!"

She gasped, her knees no longer able to support her. She sank lower on him, welcoming him against her womb.

"Come for me, Lilly."

He pinched those sensitive tips, and she shattered.

Seconds later, his own body went rigid. He pulsed against her feminine walls, sucking in a breath before spilling himself deep inside her.

Cradled in his arms, she rested on his chest.

"Thank you," he said, "for your trust."

She silently thanked him for showing her she was desirable. There would never be anything more than sex between them, no emotional connection, she knew. But that shouldn't matter; she'd soon lost the connection she'd had with her ex-husband. *It shouldn't matter.*

So why did it, suddenly?

Trying to push away the nagging thought that she might be starting to care for Nick, she relaxed against him, gulping when he reached for a pink feather and tickled her cheek with it.

"We still need to try number twenty-one."

Teasing light fired his eyes, and she'd never seen him look so carefree.

It'd be easy to lose herself in him.

And that was the one thing she dared not do....

Nine

Standing at the patio door, Lilly stared at the silvery sliver of moon and the winking stars.

The calmness of the scene should have soothed her. It didn't. A fraction of an inch at a time, control slipped away.

Above everything else in her life, she cherished being in control. She'd fought for the courage to leave Aaron, then she'd struggled through the first few months of freedom as she learned to think for herself and be independent.

Was Nick right? she wondered. Was it possible not to lose herself in him? In bed, she'd let go completely—but so had he.

From her robe pocket, she took out the lucky penny he'd given her. It touched her in a way nothing else ever had. An expensive gift wouldn't have meant as much to her as this tiny treasure. She'd keep it close, always, as a reminder that he'd thought enough of her to part with his talisman.

Silently Nick came up behind her and wrapped his arms around her.

"Can't sleep?" he asked.

"No."

"I'd give you a penny for your thoughts, but I've already given it to you."

"I know. It's in my pocket."

He kissed the side of her neck with the tenderness of a lover, and she melted against him.

"Do you want to go back to sleep?" he asked.

She turned toward him and placed her hand on his chest. "Did you have anything better in mind?" Even in the dim lighting, she saw his brow arch.

"Are you trying to seduce me, Lilly?"

"I just don't want to be alone," she admitted.

He feathered his fingers into her hair. "Want to relax in the hot tub?"

She recalled their first night together, the way they'd talked and laughed. Part of her wanted that again. "Yes."

"Ever been skinny dipping?"

"I thought you brought my bikini."

"I like looking at you, all of you."

She shivered deliciously. "I'm willing to try."

He loosened the belt holding her robe closed, dropping the ends. The material parted, and cool mountain air caressed her heated skin.

He drew the robe across her shoulders, kissing her body as he bared it. Finally, the thick terry slithered to the floor, leaving her completely naked.

Lilly opened the sliding glass door. Going outside, she was mindful that he stood inside, watching her. White lights twinkled on the pine trees, lighting the way.

She reached the water's edge and the metal railing.

"Wait."

Looking over her shoulder, she raised a brow.

"I don't want you to slip."

"I won't."

"I'm not taking chances with your safety."

With a sigh, she waited, dipping her toe in the warm water. He grabbed a couple of glasses, topped them up with their special champagne, then walked across the pool's flagstone deck.

"I'm not helpless," she told him, trying not to look at his body—flat belly, tapered waist, lean hips and powerful thighs....

"I know."

"Then—"

"Lilly, let it go," he said, putting down the glasses and descending into the water.

Because it was easier, she did. He offered his hand and she took it, accepting his guidance as he helped her.

Ruffled by their movements, the water lapped at her, and she gratefully sank onto one of the steps, enveloped up to her chin.

She tipped back her head, closing her eyes and enjoying the sensual delight of being naked and aware, under the seemingly endless Rocky Mountain night sky.

"It's quiet here," he said, the husky vibration of his voice touching a chord inside her. "A place a man can feel peace."

"Is that something you're searching for?"

He didn't answer for a long time, so long she wondered if he ever would.

"Didn't know that till I was nearly twenty-one, but yeah."

Her heart accelerated. Nick had just opened a window, offering her a glimpse at the emotions he kept locked deep inside.

Would he let her see more? she wondered. Did he trust her enough to allow her to get any closer? "You moved away for a few years."

Even though her eyes were closed, she felt the deep penetration of his stare.

"You seem to know a lot about me."

She knew he had the devil's own temper when crossed, that he was fiercely possessive and that he was determined to protect what was his—and that included her. She also knew he could be kind and considerate, putting her needs before his own. "I read Miss Starr's column," she said.

"Gossip."

She ignored the sandpapery warning that told her to back down. "She called you, Kurt and Shane Masters the Troublesome Trio."

He didn't answer.

"Was that true?"

"Probably."

"So why did you come home?"

"My mother was dying."

Bringing her head forward, Lilly looked at him.

From the dim light inside the room, as well as the moon's glow, she saw shadows lurking in his eyes.

"Kurt called me in Cheyenne, told me Mom was alone."

"After everything you'd been through, you came back to take care of her?"

"She was my mother."

"Simple as that?"

"Simple as that."

To him, it was.

He'd spent his whole childhood and the first part of his adult life telling himself no one mattered. But in that instant—when the phone rang and Kurt told him his mother was alone and dying—Nick had known the truth. Everything he'd run from caught up with him right then and there.

The same blood that ran through his veins also ran through his mother's. She'd given him life. She was the only family he had, and she was important.

No matter how far he ran, how deep he buried the past, he couldn't change who he was.

He'd never intended to tell any of this to Lilly, figuring it was no one else's business. But there was something about the way she looked at him, her lips slightly parted, her hand extended toward him on top of the water....

It was her eyes that undid him, though. The hazel flares in the green depths told him he'd touched a note inside her. She cared about him. It had been more years than he could remember since he'd felt a woman's compassion for him. Why she should, he didn't have a clue.

But he found himself opening up, exposing the deepest, darkest secrets he'd never even told Marcy. "I've been drunk three times in my life. The first was the day I left home, the second the day I came back."

Lilly reached for him.

Scooting closer, she placed her small hand on his chest, near where his heart thundered.

No woman had ever reached for him with compassion before, and it stirred a response that was far, far more than physical. It rocked him, seared him, coming from somewhere so deep it might actually have been in his soul....

"I was seventeen when I left, sick of the smell of stale sex and the sound of my mother's headboard banging against the wall. That day a man—one I'd never seen before—came out of my mom's room, must have been around noon. He wasn't wearing anything and he was scratching himself and demanding to know what the hell I was looking at.

"Mom came out of the bedroom, pulling on some clothes. We looked at each other, and I saw she was going to choose that bastard over me, like she had when I was a kid.

"I grabbed a half-empty bottle of rotgut and left. Mom didn't try and stop me, even though she had to have seen the tears I was fighting to hold back—trying to be a man."

"You were still a kid then."

"Yeah. Thought I was a grown up, though."

An owl screeched overhead, diving from a tree.

"I drove around for an hour or two, somehow ended up at Kurt's house. His dad threw me in the shower, his mom fixed me some food. Most of all, they took me in. They made me go to school and to church, forced me to do chores. The more I rebelled, the more they made me do."

"Nick..."

"It was the first time I remember anyone giving half a damn about me and what I did all day. I said I didn't want them to, but I did. It was the first time in my life I saw what love looked like. If it hadn't been for the two years I spent there, I don't think I'd have believed love even existed." Even now, he wondered if it was only meant for other people. The first woman he'd offered his heart to had kicked it and taken away the baby he adored. He knew one thing for certain: that sure as hell wasn't love.

"Ray Majors taught me about ranching, about the land. When I graduated, Alice Majors was in the bleachers, but my own mother wasn't."

Nick closed his hand around Lilly's wrist, holding onto her and the caring that she radiated. "I went to Cheyenne, got hired on at a ranch and worked my way up to foreman. What Ray didn't teach me, I learned in Wyoming."

"Then your mom got sick."

For years, this had been dormant inside, hidden, but not ever forgotten.

"Yeah. She was still in the same trailer, a rundown piece of garbage. I bought a few acres with the money I'd saved, bought a small house and moved my mother in with me."

"The same place you have now?"

"It was a lot smaller back then. Shane Masters added the second story. In the six months before she died, I got to know my mother." His lip curled. "Lived with her seventeen years, and never knew her."

"Did you ever forgive her?"

He looked at Lilly. "I understood her."

"But did you forgive her?" she pressed.

"I'm short on forgiveness." He paused.

"But the land helped us both to heal. She'd sit on the patio and stare at the mountains, said she'd never had a view like that before. And for the first time, no one expected anything from her. She had a hard life, but she told me the last few months were the best. I guess we both found peace."

"She must have been proud of the man you became."

He quirked a brow.

"I would have been," Lilly whispered.

A vise clamped around his heart. "Would you?"

"Yes," she whispered. "You learned what was important, you work hard, have honor and lots of integrity."

"Even if I'm short on forgiveness?"

"I don't believe that, Nick."

His grip on her tightened.

She shook her head, and the moisture rising from the tub made her curls cling to her cheeks. "If our child is half the person you are, I'll be proud, too."

Her words meant more to him than he could ever possibly hope to express. They filled a hollow he hadn't known existed.

He kissed her, long and deep, trying to convey what he felt and knowing it fell short. But it was all he had to offer.

He hoped it was enough.

Lilly slowly awoke, aware of Nick's arms holding her tightly, even in sleep. Her hair fanned across his bare chest, and his hand was spread across her back, his fingers pressed against her spine.

He'd made love to her twice before they fell asleep— and he'd said he liked numbers twenty-one and seventy-three equally.

She smiled. She liked them both, too.

Watery moonlight slid through the glass patio door, and the glow from the clock said it was still a couple of hours until dawn.

Beneath her ear, the rhythm of his breathing changed.

"You're supposed to be asleep," he said.

"Don't you miss anything?"

"Not when it comes to you."

She was starting to believe it, starting to like it.

"Come here," he said, moving them both until her head lay cradled in the crook of his arm.

She already knew he threatened her control, but right now, that didn't seem to matter. Right now, tonight, she wanted his comfort. Tomorrow was soon enough to worry about him being overly possessive.

He curled an arm around her, his fingers toying with her hair.

"Nick?"

"Hmm?"

"You said you had been drunk three times in your life." Would he answer?

"The third time was when my divorce was final and the judge denied me visitation rights to see Shanna."

His pain, exposed and undiluted, ripped through her like the stab of an icicle.

"Until then, I didn't believe I'd never hold her again."

Knowing him as she did now, Lilly ached.

With his honesty, the way he loved Shanna and cared for his ill mother, he'd started to work his way inside Lilly's heart.

And she had no idea what to do about it....

"Sleep," he eventually told her.

After placing a kiss on his warm skin, she finally did, wondering how she'd keep from falling in love with him.

Leaving Aaron had been difficult, but he'd never affected her as deeply, as surely, as Nick did.

Lilly dressed without turning on any lights, pulling on a pair of shorts and an oversize T-shirt. She moved around the room on tiptoe, easing the bathroom door shut and running only a small amount of water.

Not enough to wake him, she probably thought. But she had. Nick lay without moving. He wondered what she was doing, but decided to say nothing.

Without even glancing his direction, she sneaked from the room, the door shutting with a barely audible click.

His gut clenched.

Without wanting to, he thought of Marcy, the way she'd behaved, telling him one thing, doing another, spending the night away from home without calling.

But Lilly wasn't Marcy.

He knew that, but that didn't make her leaving him without a note or a word any easier to take.

Energy gnawing at him, he got up, showered and dressed. He'd killed half an hour, and she still wasn't back.

He prowled the room, imagining the sound of her sighs, the scent of her, woman and temptation, topped by an innocently floral fragrance.

She was getting to him.

He cared about her, cared where she was and what she was doing. Damn it, he wanted her here, with him. He wanted to shower her with the affection he couldn't admit to; he ached to hold her, feel her, explore her.

A key slid into the lock.

He forced himself to sit at the small table and look relaxed. Realizing he was drumming his fingers on the table, he curved his hand into a fist and held it steady.

Closing the door and juggling a package, she smiled. "Morning," she said softly.

Fear, something he hadn't realized he'd been feeling, evaporated.

"I wanted to do a little shopping," she said.

"I'd have gone with you."

"I know you would have, but I wanted to do this alone."

"Oh."

She sashayed across the carpet, holding her hand behind her back. "I got you something," she said, leaning down to feather her lips across his forehead.

"You're all I want." He pulled her onto his lap and kissed her soundly.

"Yum," she said. "Now wait, I want to give you this." She wriggled from his lap and took a box from the bag.

It was wrapped in Christmas paper sporting reindeer and a sleigh, and even had red and green ribbons, accented with a gold bow.

It had been a lot of years since he'd received a Christmas present.

Frustrating him to Montana and back, his hand shook as he slid a finger beneath the tape.

"Rip it open," she encouraged.

Inside, he found a stuffed Santa Claus.

"Since they're having Christmas in July, I was able to find this. Do you like him?"

"He's..." How did he say thanks for something that meant more than words could express? How did he say he was sorry for doubting her? "Perfect..." he murmured.

"I got him because you said you stopped believing in Santa Claus. I figured...now that we'll be having real Christmases, maybe you could believe again."

He exhaled a shaky breath. "You have no idea how much this means to me."

"I was hoping maybe you'd show me?"

He could think of nothing he'd like better.

"Will you move into my bedroom?" he asked when they arrived back at the ranch house.

The honeymoon had been too short, but if it had been any longer, she knew she would have been liable to forget how dangerous he was. Attentive to her every need, he'd been a doting groom, everything she'd ever dreamed of wanting in a husband.

But that wasn't reality.

Two nights ago, he'd opened up, honestly showing her the wounds he carried. And because she understood, knew what made him the man he was, she was doubly vulnerable to him.

And that was something she couldn't allow to happen. She'd been hurt, too, and needed to protect herself from him. Experience had taught her she was the only person she could count on. She'd vowed never to forget it.

He came around the vehicle and opened her door. "Lilly?"

His legs were spread to shoulder width and his arms were folded across his chest.

She wished she could sink into the leather seat. Instead, she unbuckled her safety belt and slid from the vehicle, forcing him to take a step back. "I'll move into your bedroom, Nick, but only because it will be less confusing for our child that way."

Two ranch hands had stopped work. Sitting on the top rail of the corral, they watched the interchange with great interest.

Nick didn't seem to care.

That was, until he took off his hat and, shielding her from their view, kissed her soundly. After ending the kiss, he said, "I just want to get inside you. It's been at least two hours."

Lost, she didn't argue when he slid his arms beneath her and carried her from the car, kicking the door shut with his heel.

Ten

"Where have you been?"

Lilly slid the bags of groceries onto the kitchen table, the lullaby she was humming drifting into silence.

After three weeks of marriage, she'd learned to recognize his stance.

The ticking pulse in his temple churned with his restrained anger, and the sting of a whiplash laced his words.

With a deep sigh, she leaned against the counter. "To town," she said unnecessarily. "Shopping. I was buying things for the nursery and getting ingredients for dinner."

He took a step toward her, then another. His heat seared her, but she tipped back her head, meeting his glance.

"We have employees who can carry groceries."

"I know."

Spurs scraping the hardwood floor, he took another step. "That is, if it didn't occur to you to ask your husband for help."

This close, she saw how hard Nick fought to control his temper. Hers flared to match it. "I didn't know I had to answer to you for every one of my moves."

"You don't."

Her eyebrows drew together in frustration. "Then...?"

"I don't want my pregnant wife hauling heavy bags around."

"It's food, Nick, not concrete."

"You could ask for help."

"I tried to find you before I left, and I couldn't. I didn't know where you were."

"And you couldn't wait?"

"No. Not if you wanted dinner on the table."

"I didn't."

"Didn't what?"

"I don't expect you to have dinner on the table when I come in."

"You don't?"

"Lilly, damn you, you—the baby—that's what's important." He devoured the rest of the space separating them. "I've lived alone most of my adult life. I can cook, I can clean, I can even do laundry." He took hold of her upper arms. "I didn't marry you to wait on me. Get this through your head—*I'm not Aaron.* You weren't married to him. You were in a trap."

"Is there a difference?" She hadn't meant to ask the question aloud, but there it was.

When she'd exchanged vows with Aaron, she hadn't realized he'd take the "obey" part so seriously. She'd loved him, wanted their relationship to work. Love hadn't been enough.

"I don't want to run your life, Lilly, and you're free to come and go anytime you want. This is a partnership, not a dictatorship." Nick exhaled deeply, and his shoulders relaxed, as if anger drained. "When you leave, I want you to write a note...not because you have to answer to me, but because it's common courtesy. And I'll leave you one when I go somewhere."

His grip on her relaxed. "Don't shut me out, Lilly. I won't let you."

"You're being unfair, Nick. I wasn't shutting you out. If you'd open your eyes, you'd see that. I need your trust. In fact, I demand it. Without it, this marriage doesn't stand a chance." After sighing, she said, "I'll leave notes in the future, but if I forget, you can't make these kind of assumptions again.

"I don't give myself to men easily. You of all people should know that."

He raked his fingers against his scalp. "Damn it, Lilly, I was worried about you."

She exhaled, seeing past her own reaction and looking into his eyes. She saw spikes of fear there. "This isn't about trust?"

"No. I was worried that you might be at the doctor's, that you might be hurt."

"I misunderstood."

"Yeah, you did. Let me help you, Lilly. Let me be your partner, not some man you're comparing me to."

She moved her fingertips down the side of his cheek, feeling the tension in his jaw. "I'm—"

"Don't apologize," he interrupted softly. "Let me welcome you home properly."

He kissed her long and deep, leaving her reeling.

When had he become so important to her? If only he returned the feelings. But she didn't dare show it, didn't dare run the risk of loving a man who would never return the feelings. For her own sake, she should continue on the

way they were. Until now, she just had no idea how difficult that might be.

"You said you were getting stuff for the nursery?"

"I bought a quilt for the crib and a stuffed toy."

"What kind of toy?"

"A Santa Claus," she said. "So that our baby will always believe, too."

"With a mom like you, how could our child *not* believe?"

Together, they went upstairs and added her purchases to
the nursery they'd started to redecorate. He hadn't com-
plained once when they looked at wallpaper samples,
lamps, furniture, even blankets.

When she suggested they do anything that had to do
with their baby, he always agreed. If her first husband had
cared a fraction as much, she would never have left him.

"While I was in town, I also stopped in at the flower
shop."

His hand was curved around the crib railing.

"Beth's swamped."

"And?"

"I'm thinking of going back to work."

"I'd prefer you didn't."

"This is a partnership," she reminded him, digging her
hands into her shorts' pocket and finding his lucky penny.
"Not a dictatorship."

"Damn it, Lilly. I don't like it."

"I'm sorry, Nick. I really didn't think you'd like the
idea."

"But that's not going to change your mind?"

She shook her head gently. "No."

A thousand different emotions pushed through him. He
didn't want her running herself ragged.

She worked hard at the flower store, carrying heavy

things, standing on her feet all day. No. He definitely didn't like it.

"This was how it started," she said softly, "with Aaron."

"Not another word," Nick warned, the words a low growl from his gut.

"This is important to me," she said. "It's my business, something I love doing. If you mean it, that this is a partnership, then you have to understand I can't just walk away from the shop without looking back."

"I'm not asking you to. You can go back right after the baby's born."

"Nick, I can't stay home all day. I'll go crazy."

"Then work for me."

"What?"

"You can do my books, take over ordering supplies, help with the administrative side of running the ranch."

"Nick—"

"Lilly, listen—"

"In our marriage vows, you said you wouldn't ask me to give up who I am. Remember?" Without another word, she left the room.

He heard her on the stairs, then the sound of her closing him out of their bedroom.

He just prayed it wasn't the start of her closing him out of her life, the way Marcy had done.

This time, he wouldn't be so blind. With Marcy, he'd been wrapped up in eking a living from the land, working eighteen hour days, falling into bed exhausted. He hadn't paid attention to the hour she left or the time she returned. The more she was gone, the more he'd withdrawn, until she ended up sleeping with another man.

He wouldn't allow that to happen with Lilly. Their marriage meant too much.

So how did he learn to compromise, without losing?

Lunch was a good place to start, he decided the next day.

He returned to the ranch house at noontime, surprised to notice how quiet it was without her.

How *lonely* it was without her.

Lonely? Hell, it wasn't lonely. He'd never been lonely his entire life. Wasn't about to start now.

But that didn't mean he wasn't married.

He drove into town, stopping by the Chuckwagon and hoping to sweet-talk Bridget into making him a picnic basket to go.

"Men. Think they can get a woman to do anything, if'n they just ask nice enough."

"Does it work?" he asked hopefully.

"I'm supposin' it might," she grumbled. "Next time, mind you, I'd like a bit of a warning. I do have other customers, you know."

When she gave him the basket—one like she used for special occasions—he surprised them both by kissing her on the cheek.

She brandished a wooden spoon with a beaming smile. "Go on with you."

When he arrived at Rocky Mountain Flowers, it was to find Lilly talking to a customer, a false smile on her tired face. She'd slipped off her shoes and her shoulders were slightly slumped.

Grinding his teeth, he said nothing.

When she looked up and saw him, her exhaustion faded. She smiled, and it lit her eyes with hazel flecks. A physical response tightened his insides, making him instantly ready.

A few minutes later, he was alone with his wife.

"Brought you some lunch."

"How'd you know I'd be hungry?"

"Lucky guess."

"There's a break room in the back. We can eat there."

She didn't even get to eat half a sandwich before the bell on the front door jingled.

"Can't people grow their own damn flowers?"

"Nick! Behave yourself. I'll be back in a few minutes."

Impatiently he waited.

"Your blouse is starting to get tight across the front," he observed a few minutes later.

"Guess I'll need to buy some new clothes."

"New bras, too?"

"Didn't I tell you to behave?"

"Me? I was just offering to take you shopping, as long as you're willing to model."

"You're impossible."

He grinned. "Yeah. Now sit and eat."

She took the chair across from him, and he reached for her feet, pulling them onto his lap and rubbing them.

Closing her eyes, she sighed contentedly.

"New shoes are a good idea," she said a few minutes later. "Maybe pants, too."

"When do you want to go?"

"Shopping?" she asked, still nearly purring. "You're not serious?"

"Sure."

"Men don't like to go shopping," she said.

"I'll pick you up at four."

"I get off at five."

"I'll pick you up at four," he reiterated.

"You're being impossible again."

"You wouldn't know what to do with me if I wasn't."

"Maybe you're right," she agreed.

He was glad he came at four. Exhaustion had sapped all

her color, and her smile was more delicate than an orchid petal. "I'm taking my wife home," he told Beth.

"I told her to go home two hours ago. She's stubborn."

"Never noticed."

"Thought we were going shopping," Lilly said when he headed for the outskirts of town.

"Thought it would be better if you rested."

"Anyone ever tell you you're bossy?"

Nick smiled. "Maybe a time or two."

By the time they arrived home, she was fighting to keep her eyes open.

"We can eat in the living room," he said.

"What do you want me to fix for dinner?"

"Got it handled," he said. "Tomato soup, from a can, and grilled cheese sandwiches."

"Sounds like heaven. You're a man after my heart, Nick."

Maybe he was. And he wondered if he'd ever get it.

"You don't need any help?"

"Told you I could cook," he said.

"But you never said you were a gourmet."

He smiled. If he'd been picking women to have his baby, he couldn't have done a much better job.

After dinner her eyelids drooped, and he sent her off to the bathtub. He gave her a few minutes of privacy before impatience rattled him.

He knocked on the door, and without waiting for an answer, went in.

She lounged against the rim, and now that she'd washed off her makeup, he saw the shadows lurking beneath her eyes. She was working too hard, damn it, and he didn't know what in the name of God's fertile earth he was supposed to do about it.

He'd never felt more helpless, and that led to frustration.

What he wouldn't give to wrap her in a cocoon of rest and relaxation. Instead, he did what he could, tamping down his natural—bossy—urges.

"Lean forward," he said, reaching for a bar of soap. "I'll wash your back."

"You're spoiling me."

"You deserve it."

She sighed softly, and he noticed the way a damp tendril of her hair curved across her nape. As if hypnotized, he lifted the curl and kissed the wet skin.

"Oh, Nick."

He adjusted the front of his jeans. Just touching her aroused him. He shoved aside the nagging voice that told him it went beyond physical attraction, that it was something deeper than her carrying his child that drew him to her.

"Time for bed," he said.

"I'm already half-asleep."

He knew. He grabbed a fluffy towel from the linen closet. Holding it with one hand, he reached for her with the other.

"I could get to like this attention."

"So could I," he said. "So could I."

Instead of just wrapping her in the terry cloth, he dried her.

Her breath caught in her throat when he rubbed the nubby material across her nipples. Instantly they responded, hardening, thickening, reaching toward him. With a gentle squeeze, he closed his thumb and forefinger around a sensitive tip. "Are you going to breast-feed?"

"I want to."

The idea of his child suckling at her trustingly, with complete love, stole his breath.

"What do you think?"

"Me?"

She blushed, color flooding her cheeks. "It'll be your baby, too."

"If you wanted to just bottle-feed, that would be okay."

"But...?"

With tenderness, he cupped her breasts, delighting in their feel, the heaviness, the changes his child brought to her body. "I thank you for wanting to do that for our baby." He kissed her breasts, but when she shivered, he knew he needed to dry her completely.

He toweled her abdomen, noting the contours weren't quiet as flat as they had been before. "You're showing more and more."

"You sound..."

"Proud. Honored."

"We'll see if you feel that way in a few months, when I'm too big to tie my own shoes."

"More so," he said. "And I'll tie them for you." Dropping to his knees, he dried her between the legs, then *there,* making her squirm.

"I didn't know—"

He looked up at her.

"—that getting dry could be such a sensual experience."

He hadn't, either.

He hadn't known, either, how much he liked caring for another human being. After Marcy left, taking Shanna from his life, he'd sworn he'd never be vulnerable again. Now he wasn't so sure.

"Bedtime," he said.

"But it's not even dark."

"And you're not tired?"

She pulled the pins from her hair, letting the silky brown

strands fall around her face. "Maybe just a little," she admitted.

In their room, he took out her nightgown and pulled it over her head.

"You don't want to make love?" she asked around a yawn.

"Yeah. I do." Just her mention of it had him thrusting against his zipper. "Tomorrow." He wondered when he'd become so noble.

He tucked her in, and he swore she fell asleep smiling.

Restless energy churned inside him and he went outside, saddled Shadow and rode west, letting the sunset draw him. He waited to feel the familiar comfort of the land, but it didn't come.

Instead, thoughts of Lilly surrounded him. The scent of her, of lavender and hope. The sound of her climax, short bursts of breath, his name whispered in his ear. And the way her body responded to his touch, her legs wavering and her hands reaching for him…

She made him glad to have found her.

And she made him harder than the earth beneath Shadow's hooves.

Nick didn't know what the hell he was going to do about his Lilly. For the first time in his life, he had more questions than answers, and they all centered on one thing: how not to lose the most important person in his life.

If he enforced his will on her, she'd see him as overbearing and controlling, ruining any hope of a long-term relationship. But he couldn't sit back and watch while she worked herself into exhaustion.

How could he make Lilly understand that he cared about her every bit as much as the baby?

That thought burned like a branding iron.

He reined in, gripping the leather with white knuckles.

They wouldn't be together if it wasn't for the baby. Sure, she made his blood run hot, but that was all. Beyond great sex and their mutual obligation, they meant nothing to each other.

Shadow nickered in disbelief.

Nick scowled.

He'd never intended to care for Lilly, hadn't wanted to care for anyone, ever again. He'd had enough experience with that to last him a couple of lifetimes. But there it was, plain and undeniable, no matter how far or fast he ran.

He wanted his child, but he cared for Lilly.

Those realizations didn't change anything, they just complicated his life further.

Lilly didn't want a real relationship. More than once, she'd made that clear.

So that left him...where?

Confused and confounded, he decided, exhaling deeply in the Colorado dusk. Somewhere along the line, things had gotten complicated.

No closer to an answer now than when he'd ridden out an hour ago, he returned home, to find Lilly awake and waiting for him. Silently, she reached for his belt, then his zipper, then him.

Liking this bold Lilly, he communicated with his body what he couldn't with words—that he cared for her and didn't intend to let her go.

"I can drive to work myself," she said, sliding her cup of decaf onto the counter.

"I know you can," he said.

After this many weeks of marriage, Lilly was able to read him as if he were one of the books she loved so much. The set of his chin told her she could argue all day long and it would get her nowhere. His mind was made up.

Well, this time, so was hers. "Thanks," she said, crossing the room and stroking his cheek with her index finger. She paused at the cleft in his chin. "But I know how much work you have to do."

His eyes narrowed and blue icicles warned of danger. "Nice try," he said, capturing her finger and closing his hand around it. He drew her finger to his mouth and sucked on it.

She should have known better…should have known nothing but honesty worked with Nick. Now, with him suckling on her the way he'd drawn a nipple into his mouth last night, heat wrapped around her womb, and neediness exploded. "We…" Where were the words and why wouldn't her tongue work?

He raised a brow.

"We should be, er…"

He let her go. His voice husky with seduction, he suggested, "Be upstairs, having sex?"

"Going," she managed to answer. "To work." How did he do that—make her forget everyone, everything, but him?

"We?"

She didn't think she was capable of driving right now. Nodding, she reached for her purse and headed toward the door.

His self-satisfied chuckle followed her down the hallway.

"Four o'clock?" he asked her when he pulled up in front of the flower store.

"Five."

He raised a brow.

"Five," she said, climbing out and slamming the door before he could respond.

"Your husband irritating you again?" Beth asked.

"Isn't he always?"

Beth snipped the stem of a sunflower. "Except for when he has you grinning like a fool."

Lilly frowned and grabbed an apron, cinching the waist. She didn't have as much string left over as she had just a couple of weeks ago.

"Same argument?" Beth guessed.

"He's a control freak."

"And you're not?"

Lilly folded her arms across her chest. "What's that supposed to mean?"

"Oh, hon, even I know you're working too hard." Beth put the bright sunflower in a vase. "We can hire more help, take some of the responsibility off you."

"I'm not quitting."

"No one asked you to. But you don't have to be here from opening until closing."

"It's half my business, too."

"But it doesn't have to run you ragged. Take some time off, enjoy your husband."

That was half the problem. She did enjoy her husband, to the point that it frightened her. She'd given her heart once, only to have her hopes and dreams crushed. She didn't dare lose control again.

"Nick's not Aaron."

"You're right. He's worse."

Beth shook her head. "Anyone can see he's head over heels about you."

"He wants his baby. He's made it clear I could leave him, as long as I don't take the baby."

"You don't think he'd go after you?"

Lilly thought of Marcy, the way he'd turned his back and never looked back. "No."

"Then, honey, you don't have eyes."

Beth's words stayed with Lilly for the next couple of hours, until they got so busy she couldn't think.

She worked through lunch, noticing the oppressive heat building in the shop, as well as inside her.

Scooping her hair from her neck, she wrapped it in a ponytail holder, then went back to helping customers and arranging Bernadette Simpson's weekly bouquet for the post office.

Lilly's feet ached, her pants cut into her expanding waistline and sweat dotted her brow.

But she still had work to do when Nick arrived.

"You're exhausted," he said, folding his arms and standing in front of her with his legs spread.

"A little tired," she admitted.

He scowled. "Let's go, Lilly."

"But I'm not done here."

"You're done."

Beth came from the back room and he turned to her. "I'm taking your sister home. And she won't be in tomorrow."

"No problem."

Frustration simmered, like a kettle on slow boil. "I'm not leaving," Lilly said.

"Willingly or in my arms. Choice is yours. But you're coming home."

She gasped. "You're not serious!"

"Try me."

Beth smothered a grin behind her hand. "I'll deliver the post office arrangement," she said. "Just go home with your husband."

Nick held open the door.

Lilly seethed.

Refusing to have a scene in public, she grabbed her

purse and strode to the car, her footsteps echoing off the boardwalk planks.

"Anyone ever tell you you're the most stubborn, obstinate person in the world?" he asked, sliding in beside her and pinning her with an icy stare.

"Me?" she demanded. "You've got room to talk."

"And we will—talk."

"You're right," she fired back, "it's time we got a few things straight, Nick Andrews."

Tension hung thick as blinding snow, churning her insides.

At home, she didn't wait for him to come around and open the car door.

He strode into the house behind her and tossed his Stetson on the counter. She had a clear view of the angry pulse ticking in his temple, and she saw the tight line of his set lips.

Her stomach muscles contracted. This argument had been brewing for a while. And one thing was certain, she couldn't allow Nick to dictate her life.

"Sit down," he snapped.

"I prefer to stand."

"And I prefer you sit. Now."

She stood.

He paced the kitchen floor with determined, powerful strides. Each step increased her inner turmoil until it simmered just beneath the surface.

"You can work half days," he said, stopping only inches from her. His scent, that of mountain air and anger, hung like a cloud. "No more."

She froze. "Half days?" she managed to gasp. "Just who do you think you are?"

"Your husband—a man who's willing to compromise. I really don't want you working, period."

"Forget it, Nick."

He grabbed hold of her shoulders. "I will not have my wife working herself to the bone to prove some ridiculous point."

She shoved him away and strode to the far side of the room.

"You want to prove you can handle it, that you're not lazy, that you're some kind of superwoman. Let me tell you, Lilly Andrews, you're married now. To me. You're not Superwoman, and you don't have to be."

"I am not giving up my job."

"I didn't ask you to," he said in clipped tones. "But anyone can see you're beyond tired, have been ever since we got back from our honeymoon. You've got shadows beneath your eyes, your forehead was beaded with sweat when I got to the shop. You're running yourself into the ground, and I won't stand for it. Lady, you've reached the end of my patience."

"And you've reached the end of mine," she retorted. "You want me here, because you think it's best. You're telling me it's for my own good, and next you'll have me believe that I'd be better off not working at all. You want me completely dependent on you." She tipped up her chin. "Forget it."

In that instant, his temper blazed. She saw the flare singe his eyes.

"How dare you compare me to that moron you married. This isn't about control. You have your own money, your own accounts, and you're an authorized signer on every one of mine." He dragged his hand through his hair. "This is about you—the way you're working so hard when you should be taking care of yourself."

"This is about your baby," she countered. "You refuse to lose another child, and you're taking it out on me."

He strode across the kitchen and clamped his hands on her shoulders. "Damn it, Lilly, is it so hard for you to realize I care about you?"

"Use all the sweet words you want, Nick. I know the truth. You'll do anything—say anything—as long as you win."

Her insides ached. Somewhere along the line, she'd started to care for the tough and tender Nick. She didn't want this to be about their child, but she would be an idiot if she believed otherwise. Loving Nick would be impossible. He'd never return the emotion, and he'd use it against her, like Aaron had.

The aftermath of the explosion settled like shrapnel, most of it embedded in her heart.

Then quietly, but with the force of a whiplash, he said, "Maybe this marriage happened because of my baby...but are you going to deny the sexual attraction that conceived our child?"

"Nick—"

"And what about the way we make love? You called out my name last night, and I spilled myself deep inside you, against your womb. Did you forget that?"

She shivered.

"This is only about the baby?" he asked softly. "So why did you reach for my belt the other night after my ride? Are you denying that I can make you sexually hungry?"

A furious blush flashed across her face.

"And what about the way we each talk about our day after I pick you up from work? No friendship has developed between us?"

"I have a lot of friends."

"But only one lover."

She couldn't breathe, couldn't think.

He was right, she only had one lover…him. No other man possessed the same power over her that Nick did. No other man could control her, make her want things she'd sworn she'd never want again.

No other man had stolen her heart.

No other man spelled danger the way Nick did.

Nick, though, had dug a well of emotion deep inside her soul. If she allowed him to stay any longer, she'd never survive without his love.

That threat nipping at her, she shoved off his grip.

"Lilly!"

She grabbed hold of the door, twisting the knob and yanking it open.

"Lilly, wait!"

Running from him in panic—and from herself—she raced across the land, needing air, needing space, needing to be away from him.

Her tears blinding her, Lilly didn't see the piece of downed timber until it was too late.

Eleven

Nick sprinted to her side and dropped to his knees. "Are you okay?"

She sobbed hysterically, reaching for him and wrapping her arms around his neck. She hadn't expected him to react with anything but anger.

Instead, she found his gentleness.

He cradled her, offering promises that everything would be okay, promises she clung to through her panic.

"I'm sorry," she whispered. Terror numbed her insides. What if she miscarried? She'd never thought she would be a mother; now her own foolishness might cost her that chance.

Sobs wracked her body. What if she lost Nick, too? Self-preservation instincts had blinded her to the reality of what she had—Nick. She loved him, but instead of finding that comforting, she'd allowed it to paralyze her. Now, faced with the possibility of losing everything, she realized how important it all was. Reaching toward his furrowed brow, she said, "I'm so, so sorry."

"I know, Lilly, I know."

In that moment, she believed he did.

"Where does it hurt?"

"I just feel jarred," she said.

"We've still got to get you to the doctor."

She nodded, needing his reassurance.

"It'll be fine," he said.

She clung to those words as well as his lucky penny through the agonizingly long drive into town.

When they arrived, Nick carried her into the office, the antiseptic smell stinging his nose and tightening his gut. Never breaking stride, he clipped an order to the nurse, telling her to get the doctor immediately.

They were shown into an examination room, and Nick helped Lilly change into the cloth gown.

Less than a minute later, Dr. Johnson hurried in, instructing Nick to wait outside.

She gulped, wanting, needing Nick's calming presence.

He held her hand for a few seconds, squeezing it before tucking her hair behind her ear. "It'll be okay," he swore again.

"Outside, young man," Dr. Johnson reiterated.

Until now, Nick had never known bone-deep terror.

The door shut, sealing Lilly—and her wide-eyed fear—from his view.

He paced the waiting room, his boots gnawing at the floor as agitation swarmed through him. Minutes later, he stopped and slammed his closed fist against the wall, swearing silently.

A thousand thoughts crowded his mind. He didn't want to lose the baby—God knew he couldn't survive it.

But more, he didn't want to lose Lilly.

The idea of life without her loomed as dark as a moonless mountain night.

When his first marriage had ended and a judge had sided against him, Nick had vowed never to open his heart ever again. But Lilly, with her fiery independence, had sneaked inside without him even realizing it.

He'd meant it when he told her his demands were about her and not just their child. He'd been fighting it for days, if not weeks.

There was something about Lilly, with her grin, her sensual response and caring nature, that plowed past all his defenses. A mixture of innocence and passion, she aroused him.

He rapped his knuckles on the wall, ignoring the stares of a nurse and the receptionist.

He loved Lilly.

Plain and simple, and complicated as hell, he loved her.

The thought was as foreign as it was unwelcome. But the more he pushed it away, the stronger it became.

He was fooling himself when he admitted only to caring for her. He cherished her, her dedication to their child, her job. Even the things that drove him the craziest, he admired. "I love her," he said aloud.

"Of course you do, Mr. Andrews," the receptionist said.

Why hadn't he seen it before now?

He'd been attracted to her at Kurt and Jessie's wedding, and now, knowing Lilly, he had no doubt she honestly believed he didn't want to be a father. Open and honest, she didn't have a deceptive bone in her body.

In comparing her to the lying, betraying Marcy, he'd jumped to the wrong conclusions. Having an affair would be as foreign to Lilly's nature as it would be to his.

She hadn't wanted their marriage, but she'd made the most of it, doing what was right.

This was a woman who could love and be loved, a woman he could trust with his innermost secrets, a woman who still carried his lucky penny and who hadn't laughed when he'd given it to her. This was a woman who thought of others first, who cared that he didn't believe in Santa Claus, and wanted their child to always believe.

Nick had been so blinded by his own past that he hadn't seen that their moral compasses pointed the same direction.

He exhaled sharply, sinking into one of the uncomfortable vinyl seats, feet planted on the scarred floor.

She'd been right in accusing him of trying to control her. He was so desperate to ensure he didn't lose another child, he'd threatened Lilly with the most powerful weapon in his arsenal, a custody suit.

From the first, he'd been determined to have his way. Hung up on that, he hadn't even admitted the truth to himself—that even before their wedding, Lilly mattered to him every bit as much as the baby.

And now…he loved her, would do anything to keep her.

He vowed to tell her as soon as he could hold her, risk be damned. He wanted her as his wife, in an emotional as well as physical way—forevermore.

"You can come in now, young man," Dr. Johnson said.

Nick rushed through the door, striding to where she sat on the table. He took her hand in his. "I love you, Lilly," he said, the words pulsing with pure honesty. "Tell me you're okay."

"I—you—"

"Mother and baby are both fine," the doctor said, clearing his throat. "I'll leave the two of you alone."

The doctor left, and a smile lit up Nick's face. The news that they were both fine spilled light into his soul.

"I'm sorry," she said, eyes wide, glistening with unshed tears, "for scaring you. For running."

He placed his finger on her lips and shook his head. "You were right."

With a trembling hand, she brushed errant strands of hair back from her forehead.

"*I* was wrong," he added.

"No."

"You can continue to work, and I'll do what I can to support that in every way. You don't have to give up anything. I'll hire extra hands, a nanny if you want me to. Whatever you dream, I'll support you. As long as you'll come home to me at the end of each day."

"You still want me to?"

He scowled. "Of course I want you to."

"You're not angry with me?"

He squeezed her hand and looked into her eyes, deeply. "I'm angry with myself."

"I don't understand."

"You were right when you said I wanted to control you. I wanted you home, relaxing, taking care of yourself and the baby. It was about what I wanted, not what was best for you."

She exhaled deeply.

"I thought I might lose the baby," she whispered hoarsely. Luminescent tears chased the verdant green from her eyes, leaving them hazel. "And if I lost the baby, I might lose you, too."

"You wouldn't," Nick assured her.

"What are you saying?"

"I want our marriage to be forever."

"Even if—"

"Even if there wasn't going to be a baby, I'd want us to stay together."

She was afraid to hope. "Did you mean it, that…?"

"Yes. I love you, Lilly. I'm willing to change, be the kind of husband you want."

Shaking her head, she said, "I don't want you to change."

His pulse lurched.

Tears swarmed her eyes, but this time, they were tears of joy. "You love me?" she whispered incredulously.

"Yeah. With my heart and soul."

He loved her.

Her.

She was so sure she'd never be loved, certain she'd live the rest of her life as an outsider in her own marriage.

She'd fought hard, determined not to fall in love. Then, when it was too late and she'd already surrendered her heart, she'd tried to bury her vulnerability where he'd never see it.

A tear spilled, splashing on his hand. "It was me who couldn't see," she said, her voice shaky. "I let the scars that Aaron left behind blind me."

The two men couldn't have been more different. Nick didn't want her to wait on him hand and foot, never even asked her to quit work. Instead, he'd asked her to consider working part-time, so that she could rest more.

He'd never insisted she prepare his dinner; in fact, most times he cooked for her. He quit work early every day to pick her up at the flower shop, turning his dreams over to someone else in order to care for her. "You were right when you said there's a big difference between control and caring." And now she saw where that line was drawn—down the middle of his heart.

She didn't have anything to prove. Nick would never try to form her into the image of someone he wanted her to be. She could fulfill her dreams of being a mother, knowing her husband supported her completely. "You once said I could work for you. Does the offer still stand?"

"With your help, the ranch will be more productive."

"And it's okay if I want to work part-time at the store?"

"As long as I get to spoil you when you're home."

Her soul soared.

With hesitation between each word, he asked her, "Do you love me?"

She met the intensity in his eyes, responding to it deep inside. "Yes, Nick. I love you. I've loved you since our honeymoon, from the moment you let me set the pace."

"I swear to love, cherish, trust, protect and pamper you, and above all, honor you," he said, raising her hand and placing it over his heart. "Will you be my lifelong wife?"

Shaking with the enormity of her commitment, she said, "Yes."

Taking her in his arms and holding her close, he sealed the agreement with a kiss that ignited every nerve ending. She responded with everything she had to offer—her honesty, her passion, her love....

His blue eyes were twinkling when he pulled back and said, "I want to take my wife home."

"I want that, too."

"Your wish is my command," he said, sweeping her from the table and holding her tightly against his chest.

After she dressed, they left the room, his fingers possessively pressed against her spine.

"We're in love," he told Dr. Johnson on their way out of the office.

"I'd say so," the older man said dryly, smiling.

"Hey, Bernadette," Nick called to the postmistress when they were outside, "can you get a message to Miss Starr?"

The prim and proper woman patted the bun tucked at her nape. "She usually has a way of hearing things."

"Tell her Lilly's favorite flowers are now red tulips."

"Oh, I see."

Lilly laughed. Even though she laid her fingers on Nick's mouth, she couldn't get him to be quiet.

"And tell her Lilly's no longer reading books with tragic endings."

"Miss Starr will be tickled pink," Bernadette said, pressing her hands together and smiling.

"You're impossible, Mr. Andrews," Lilly said as he eased her onto the vehicle's leather seat.

"You've got a lifetime to straighten me out, Mrs. Andrews."

"I might need a bit longer than that."

"Lady, you can have as long as you want."

Then, obviously not caring who was looking, Nick captured her chin, then her lips, whispering words of love.

Epilogue

Miss Starr sat in the front row of the town's whitewashed church, clutching a lace handkerchief. On Sundays she sat in the back row, so that she could watch everyone, but today was Christmas Eve, and she didn't want to miss a thing.

Nick, Lilly and brand-new baby Noelle were part of the church's first ever Christmas pageant, representing a Colorado Christmas. And the precious little infant hadn't even let out a single peep.

Lilly and Nick knelt on either side of the rustic wooden cradle, Nick's battered cowboy hat unable to hide the fact he had eyes only for his wife and baby.

The three wise men, Kurt Majors, Shane Masters and Sheriff Spencer McCall, each wore chaps and hats, as if they'd ridden long and hard to reach the church in the six inches of fresh snow. Each of them brought a gift to the baby—a gold nugget, sage, and a bough made from fresh evergreen.

While they were each presenting the baby with their presents, Miss Starr slipped from her pew, placing a sprig of baby's breath near the cradle.

After all, Miss Starr thought, she'd had a big part in bringing the Andrews family together, and love was the greatest gift of all.

As the minister, Reverend Matthew Sheffield, finished narrating the Christmas story, Miss Starr couldn't help but look at the three wise men. Kurt was happily married, judging by the expression on his face as his eyes sought Jessie in the crowd. Spencer was the law in the town and had decided that a badge and romance didn't mix. Miss Starr would have to see about that.

And then there was Shane Masters. He'd been married once, head over heels in love, if her aging mind still served her, which it most certainly did. She'd learned yesterday that Shane's ex-wife was returning to town in the next couple of weeks to take over her aunt's cappuccino and gift store.

Should be interesting, she thought, dabbing her teary eyes with the scrap of lace.

Two of the Troublesome Trio were now living their own happily ever afters, and she reckoned it was time that the third got a ring on his finger, too.

Maybe there was something she could do to help there, too. After all, there was definitely an advantage to being the postmistress. She was usually the first to know things, giving her plenty of opportunity to get Cupid in place. Yes, indeedy.

She joined the congregation in singing "We Wish You a Merry Christmas" as the three wise men led the procession back up the aisle.

When Nick and Lilly followed with newborn Noelle tenderly cradled against her mother's breast, Miss Starr's gaze connected with Lilly's.

The warmth of Lilly's radiant smile made Miss Starr's sixty-something-year-old heart miss a couple of beats. Oh, to be in love again...

Nick tenderly placed a kiss on Lilly's forehead, and Miss Starr couldn't help but smile as she joined in the resounding chorus to the song.

In the lobby, Kurt and Jessie sought out Nick and his family. Lilly and Jessie cooed over Noelle, and Nick asked Kurt, "When are you having a baby of your own?"

"Maybe soon," he said.

Nick raised a brow.

"It's too soon to tell. But I'll let you know."

He congratulated his friend. Then he grinned when Kurt asked about Nick's marriage. "You were right. It's not just about convenience."

Kurt grinned. "Figured so." After he'd helped his wife into a down parka, they said their good-nights and headed into the Christmas snow.

On their way out of the sanctuary, Beth and her parents stopped, reminding Nick and Lilly what time they were expected for Christmas dinner.

"We'll be there, Mrs. Baldwin," Nick promised.

"Mom," the woman corrected.

"Mom?"

"If you don't mind calling me that, I don't mind, either."

His heart gave a funny little skip. A real mom? He hardly knew what to say. Kissing her on the cheek, he said, "I'd be honored."

"Still don't believe in Santa?" Lilly asked.

"I'm starting to," he confessed. Beginning with Lilly and Noelle and continuing with a real family Christmas, all his dreams were coming true.

Shane Masters took off his hat and slapped it against his dusty chaps before saying good-night.

"Would you like to join us for dinner tomorrow?" Lilly invited.

Was there no end to the joy she brought to his life? Nick wondered. Always generous, she was even inviting his single friends for Christmas dinner.

"No, thanks. Bridget at the Chuckwagon gave me a care package. I'll have plenty of food tomorrow."

"You'll be all alone?" Lilly asked, horrified.

"Don't mind," he said. "Gives me a chance to catch up on some work. Congratulations on your beautiful baby."

Without another word, he, too, disappeared.

Finally, they were alone, except for Reverend Sheffield. "I have a favor to ask," Nick said.

"Sure thing."

"I'd like to recite my vows again, in front of you."

Matt nodded.

"Adding the promise to love my wife, till death do us part."

"Couldn't think of anything more appropriate."

With a few promptings from Matt, Nick managed his vows again, this time offering them from the heart and with trust.

Then, making his spirits soar, Lilly did the same.

An hour later, they were alone, at home, wrapped in the tradition and magic of Christmas Eve.

Nick was holding his infant and staring with wonder into her perfect little face.

She looked back, eyes wide with pure love. Her tiny

hand wound around his much larger index finger as she blinked up at him.

"I've been blessed by miracles, Lilly," he whispered. "Thank you."

She padded over, her bare feet swallowed by the carpeting in the nursery. Rubbing his forearm, her heart melting, she said, "I love you more each day."

And she did.

She'd worked at the flower shop an hour a day and had taken over doing the ranch's books, almost up until the time she went into labor with Noelle. Nick never tried to tie her down or hold her back, and her soul seemed to open up more every day.

And now that she was a wife and a mommy... Her heart skipped a beat. She'd never been happier.

She wasn't content to let it rest at that. She tried, every day, in every way, to be the kind of wife he deserved, loving him with everything she had to offer.

Together, they lay Noelle in her crib. By unspoken agreement, they stood arm in arm, watching their child sleep, looking at her during the sacred moments that led to midnight and their first Christmas as a family. And in her pocket, Nick's talisman rested, a symbol of his love.

"Merry Christmas, darling," Nick said softly against Lilly's ear.

All her responses stirred, the way they always did when she was in his arms. "There's mistletoe near the fireplace."

"What are we waiting for?" He grinned and led her downstairs, where the white star on top of the tree seemed to offer the same promise of love that it had for nearly two thousand years.

There were presents there for all, as he'd always dreamed—a perfect holiday with his family.

Outside the living room window, snow drifted into fluffy white banks, decorating the landscape and clinging to a wagon wheel they'd decorated together.

"Thanks for the flowers," she said, admiring the pots of lilies he'd sent her—telling her it was heaven to be with her. He hadn't been content to have just lilies delivered to the hospital; she'd also received a dozen red roses and a bouquet of red tulips.

He'd remembered that she'd never received flowers and had taken care of that in a huge way.

"I know it's too soon to make love yet," he said wickedly. "But I have a few ideas we could try, to celebrate."

"Oh?" she asked innocently.

Whispering a very naughty, "Ho, ho, ho," he reached for her. Reverently he unwrapped *her,* the greatest gift he'd ever received.

* * * * *

Desire®

These women are about to find out what happens
when they are forced to wed the men of their dreams
in **Silhouette Desire's** new series promotion:

The Bridal Bid

Look for
the bidding to begin
in **December 1999** with:

GOING...GOING...WED! (SD #1265)
by **Amy J. Fetzer**

And look for
THE COWBOY TAKES A BRIDE (SD#1271)
by **Cathleen Galitz** in **January 2000:**

Don't miss the next book in this series,
MARRIAGE FOR SALE (SD #1284)
by **Carol Devine,** coming in **April 2000.**

The Bridal Bid only from **Silhouette Desire**.

Available at your favorite retail outlet.

Silhouette®

™ *Where love comes alive*™

Visit us at www.romance.net   SDTBB2

If you enjoyed what you just read,
then we've got an offer you can't resist!

Take 2 bestselling
love stories FREE!
Plus get a FREE surprise gift!

Clip this page and mail it to Silhouette Reader Service™

IN U.S.A.	IN CANADA
3010 Walden Ave.	P.O. Box 609
P.O. Box 1867	Fort Erie, Ontario
Buffalo, N.Y. 14240-1867	L2A 5X3

YES! Please send me 2 free Silhouette Desire® novels and my free surprise gift. Then send me 6 brand-new novels every month, which I will receive months before they're available in stores. In the U.S.A., bill me at the bargain price of $3.12 plus 25¢ delivery per book and applicable sales tax, if any*. In Canada, bill me at the bargain price of $3.49 plus 25¢ delivery per book and applicable taxes**. That's the complete price and a savings of over 10% off the cover prices—what a great deal! I understand that accepting the 2 free books and gift places me under no obligation ever to buy any books. I can always return a shipment and cancel at any time. Even if I never buy another book from Silhouette, the 2 free books and gift are mine to keep forever. So why not take us up on our invitation. You'll be glad you did!

225 SEN CNFA
326 SEN CNFC

Name	(PLEASE PRINT)	
Address	Apt.#	
City	State/Prov.	Zip/Postal Code

* Terms and prices subject to change without notice. Sales tax applicable in N.Y.
** Canadian residents will be charged applicable provincial taxes and GST.
   All orders subject to approval. Offer limited to one per household.
   ® are registered trademarks of Harlequin Enterprises Limited.

DES99   ©1998 Harlequin Enterprises Limited

LINDSAY McKENNA
continues her heart-stopping series:

MORGAN'S MERCENARIES
III
THE HUNTERS

Coming in October 1999:
HUNTER'S PRIDE
Special Edition #1274

Devlin Hunter had a way with the ladies, but when it
came to his job as a mercenary, the brooding bachelor
worked alone. Then his latest assignment paired him up
with Kulani Dawson, a feisty beauty whose tender
vulnerabilities brought out his every protective instinct—
and chipped away at his proud vow never to fall in love....

Coming in January 2000:
THE UNTAMED HUNTER
Silhouette Desire #1262

Rock-solid Shep Hunter was unconquerable—until his
mission brought him face-to-face with Dr. Maggie Harper,
the woman who'd walked away from him years ago.
Now Shep struggled to keep strong-willed Maggie under
his command without giving up the steel-clad grip on
his heart....

Look for Inca's story when Lindsay McKenna continues
the MORGAN'S MERCENARIES series with a brand-new,
longer-length single title—coming in 2000!

Available at your favorite retail outlet.

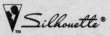

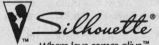

EXTRA! EXTRA!

The book all your favorite authors are raving about is finally here!

The 1999 Harlequin and Silhouette coupon book.

Each page is alive with savings that can't be beat!

Getting this incredible coupon book is as easy as 1, 2, 3.

1. During the months of November and December 1999 buy any 2 Harlequin or Silhouette books.

2. Send us your name, address and 2 proofs of purchase (cash receipt) to the address below.

3. Harlequin will send you a coupon book worth $10.00 off future purchases of Harlequin or Silhouette books in 2000.

Send us 3 cash register receipts as proofs of purchase and we will send you 2 coupon books worth a total saving of $20.00 (limit of 2 coupon books per customer).

Saving money has never been this easy.

Please allow 4-6 weeks for delivery. Offer expires December 31, 1999.

I accept your offer! Please send me (a) coupon booklet(s):

Name: _____

Address: _____ City: _____

State/Prov.: _____ Zip/Postal Code: _____

Send your name and address, along with your cash register receipts as proofs of purchase, to:

In the U.S.: Harlequin Books, P.O. Box 9057, Buffalo, N.Y. 14269

In Canada: Harlequin Books, P.O. Box 622, Fort Erie, Ontario L2A 5X3

Order your books and accept this coupon offer through our web site
http://www.romance.net
Valid in U.S. and Canada only.

PHQ4994R